That's My Baby!

"Pregnant."

Jane said the word aloud without inflection.

A simple statement for a major complication she had spent the past few weeks refusing to consider.

Somewhere in the back of her mind she had known it. But until now, she hadn't allowed herself to actually accept it. She'd told herself that surely one night of lovemaking wouldn't result in a baby. So many women her age, desperate for a child, tried to conceive for years without success.

A baby. Just in time for Christmas…

Not just *a* baby, she amended. *Her baby.*

And Max's.

Dear Reader,

The blissful days of summer may be drawing to a close, but love is just beginning to unfold for six special couples at Special Edition!

This month's THAT'S MY BABY! title is brought to you by reader-favorite Nikki Benjamin. *The Surprise Baby* is a heartfelt marriage of convenience story featuring an aloof CEO whose rigid rules about intimacy—and fatherhood— take a nosedive when an impulsive night of wedded bliss results in a surprise bundle of joy. You won't want to miss this tale about the wondrous power of love.

Fasten your seat belts! In these reunion romances, a trio of lovelorn ladies embark on the rocky road to true love. *The Wedding Ring Promise,* by bestselling author Susan Mallery, features a feisty heroine embarking on the adventure of a lifetime with the gorgeous rebel from her youth. Next, a willful spitfire succumbs to the charms of the tough-talkin' cowboy from her past in *A Family Kind of Guy* by Lisa Jackson—book one in her new FOREVER FAMILY miniseries. And in *Temporary Daddy,* by Jennifer Mikels, an orphaned baby draws an unlikely couple back together—for good!

Also don't miss *Warrior's Woman* by Laurie Paige—a seductive story about the healing force of a tender touch; and forbidden love was never more enticing than when a pair of star-crossed lovers fulfill their true destiny in *Meant To Be Married* by Ruth Wind.

I hope you enjoy each and every story to come!

Sincerely,

Karen Taylor Richman,
Senior Editor

Please address questions and book requests to:
Silhouette Reader Service
U.S.: 3010 Walden Ave., P.O. Box 1325, Buffalo, NY 14269
Canadian: P.O. Box 609, Fort Erie, Ont. L2A 5X3

NIKKI BENJAMIN

THE SURPRISE BABY

Silhouette®

SPECIAL ▼ EDITION®

Published by Silhouette Books

America's Publisher of Contemporary Romance

SILHOUETTE BOOKS

ISBN 0-373-24189-5

THE SURPRISE BABY

Copyright © 1998 by Barbara Vosbein

All rights reserved. Except for use in any review, the reproduction or utilization of this work in whole or in part in any form by any electronic, mechanical or other means, now known or hereafter invented, including xerography, photocopying and recording, or in any information storage or retrieval system, is forbidden without the written permission of the editorial office, Silhouette Books, 300 East 42nd Street, New York, NY 10017 U.S.A.

All characters in this book have no existence outside the imagination of the author and have no relation whatsoever to anyone bearing the same name or names. They are not even distantly inspired by any individual known or unknown to the author, and all incidents are pure invention.

This edition published by arrangement with Harlequin Books S.A.

® and TM are trademarks of Harlequin Books S.A., used under license. Trademarks indicated with ® are registered in the United States Patent and Trademark Office, the Canadian Trade Marks Office and in other countries.

Printed in U.S.A.

NIKKI BENJAMIN

was born and raised in the Midwest, but after years in the Houston area, she considers herself a true Texan. Nikki says she's always been an avid reader. (Her earliest literary heroines were Nancy Drew, Trixie Belden and Beany Malone.) Her writing experience was limited, however, until a friend started penning a novel and encouraged Nikki to do the same. One scene led to another, and soon she was hooked.

When not reading or writing, the author enjoys spending time with her husband and son, as well as doing needlepoint, hiking, biking, horseback riding and sailing.

Dear Reader,

No matter what our hopes and dreams may be or how carefully we plan and prepare, more often than not there is an element of surprise in becoming a parent. Listening to the advice of well-meaning friends or reading books written on the subject can smooth the way somewhat. But actually taking on the role of mommy or daddy is a unique experience marked by unexpected terrors as well as triumphs.

Yet there is nothing I consider more rewarding than guiding, teaching and encouraging a child—*your* child—to be a kind, sensitive, independent, intelligent, responsible young adult. Granted the challenges can sometimes seem overwhelming and mistakes will be made along the way, but those are givens with any great adventure. And that's exactly what parenting should be—a *most* excellent adventure.

I have had the opportunity to do many interesting and exciting things in my life. Nothing has given me quite as much joy or nearly the satisfaction as being a mother. Seems like only yesterday I was cradling my newborn son in my arms. Now he's college-bound.

Note to Jane and Max: savor every moment—time really *does* fly when you're having fun!

Chapter One

The last thing Maxwell Hamilton had planned to do on his wedding night was make love to his wife. But as he caught a glimpse of her, standing on the balcony of his penthouse apartment, gazing out into the darkness, a slight breeze swirling the hem of her calf-length, cream silk dress, his body pulsed with anticipation. The same anticipation that had first stirred somewhere deep inside him when the chaste kiss with which he had intended to seal their vows had suddenly turned into something else altogether.

When she had joined him at the altar of the tiny chapel he'd chosen for the marriage ceremony, she had looked nothing at all like *his* Ms. Elliott, vice president of marketing for Hamilton Enterprises. Wearing an old-fashioned wedding dress, her dark hair curling softly around her shoulders, she had looked so young, so lovely and so damned desirable his breath had caught in his throat.

He'd had a hard time concentrating on what the elderly minister was saying, and when the time had come to pledge his troth, there had been a roughness around the edge of his voice that had taken him by surprise.

After they'd been pronounced husband and wife, Max had turned to Jane. She'd looked up at him and smiled, and again he'd been thrown off balance. Just one kiss to seal their vows, he'd thought. One swift kiss that—in the blink of an eye—had turned into something long and slow and deep.

Something that had left them staring at each other in astonishment.

"Have the last of your guests left, sir?" Kerner inquired as he joined Max at the far end of the apartment's elegantly appointed formal living room.

Glancing at the butler, Max nodded, then raised his crystal champagne glass to his lips and drained it.

"I trust the reception went as well as you expected."

"Very well," Max replied, reaching for the open bottle on the table beside him and, against his better judgment, refilling his glass.

"Would you like me to have the staff begin tidying up?"

"Send everyone home," Max instructed, his eyes on his wife as he swirled the sparkling wine in his glass. "You can take the rest of evening off, as well. The tidying up can wait until tomorrow."

"Of course, sir," Kerner replied.

"Anything else?" Max asked, glancing at the butler, one eyebrow arched, when he failed to move away immediately.

"I hope you and Ms. Elliott will be happy together, sir."

"*Mrs. Hamilton,*" Max stated with a possessiveness that caught him by surprise.

"I'm sorry, sir. You and *Mrs. Hamilton.*"

"Thanks, Kerner. I hope so, too."

"If I may be so bold, sir…"

"Far be it from me to try to stop you," Max retorted, tossing a wry look the older man's way.

"She's a fine woman, Maxwell. A very fine woman, indeed."

"I'm glad you think so."

"What I think isn't all that important," Kerner advised. "It's what *you* think that really matters."

Feeling chastened by the butler's quiet comment, Max turned away. He raised his glass, swallowed another mouthful of champagne, then shifted uncomfortably from one foot to the other as his gaze fell upon Jane yet again.

"I'll try to keep that in mind," he answered at last, his tone brusque.

"I'm sure you will, sir."

"Good night, Kerner."

"Good night, sir."

Retrieving the almost empty champagne bottle from the table, the butler headed for the long hallway that led to the kitchen and his quarters beyond.

There were times when Calvin Kerner forgot himself and treated Max like a wayward son. Usually, Max didn't mind. They had been together almost twelve years, and during that time, Calvin had seen him at his very best and his very worst.

At his first wife's behest, Max had paid an exorbitant amount at a charity auction for one month of the butler's services. At the end of the thirty days, Calvin Kerner had become so much a part of the family that Max and Alyssa had begged the man to stay on. Since then, they had gone through a lot together. In fact, had it not been for Calvin, Max wasn't sure how he would have survived the loss of his wife and...

Don't think about that now, Max warned himself, drinking from his glass again.

He wasn't about to wallow in past misery. Not tonight. Nor was he going to allow a minor dressing-down from the one person who often seemed to know him better than he knew himself to throw him off the change in course he had set for himself and his bride.

Tonight, fortified by an excess of champagne, Maxwell Hamilton was going to do the one thing he prided himself on never doing. He was going to renege on a deal. His deal with Jane Elliott, now Jane Hamilton.

He no longer wanted their marriage to be one in name only. He wanted Jane writhing naked under him in his bed as he laid claim to what he now considered rightfully his.

Granted, he had given her the impression that he didn't expect their relationship to be of a sexual nature. But there was nothing at all in the prenuptial contract they'd signed to preclude it. Of course, he would never force her. If that kiss they'd shared at the chapel was any indication, however, he didn't think he would have to.

Setting aside his empty glass, Max started across the wide expanse of living room, moving slowly, pausing to switch off one lamp, then another along the way, the lush carpet muffling his footsteps.

As if sensing his approach, Jane glanced over her shoulder. She stared at him for a long moment, her eyes wide, then looked away. She seemed to be measuring the distance she would have to travel from the balcony to the long, narrow hallway that would take her to her bedroom, as if readying herself to make a run for it.

To her credit, she chose instead to hold her ground. And though her grasp on the balcony rail tightened perceptibly as she turned away, Max noted approvingly that she also lifted her chin and straightened her shoulders.

He had chosen well, he thought. But then, he had used his head rather than his heart once he had accepted the fact that marrying again would be to his advantage.

He had never fully recovered from the anguish he'd endured when he'd lost his wife and child seven years ago. For a very long time, he had buried himself under a mountain of paperwork, slaving at the office day and night, returning to the apartment as little as possible and seeing no one other than his employees.

Gradually, however, he had come to realize that as CEO of the multinational computer-manufacturing company he had built up over the past fifteen years, he had social responsibilities to fulfill, as well. Responsibilities that wouldn't be quite so burdensome with a woman by his side.

Not one of the horde of sweet young things intent on clipping his wings, but a mature, sensible woman who wouldn't expect the kind of hearts-and-flowers romance he was no longer capable of offering. A woman worthy of his respect who was willing to serve as his trusted companion. A woman who could accept her place in his life with equanimity.

Jane Elliott had immediately come to mind.

Six years ago, after completing her MBA at Stanford University, she had taken a job in the company's marketing department. Her bright, innovative ideas had impressed everyone, including Max. She had risen through the ranks, taking on more and more responsibility. Then, about eighteen months ago, the head of the department decided to take early retirement. Jane had been the natural choice to take his place. Max had offered her the job, she had accepted and never once had he regretted it.

They had worked closely together on the marketing of a new line of software shortly after her promotion, so they had already established a cordial relationship when he'd begun to think of marrying again. Discreetly worded inquiries had revealed nothing to change his high opinion of her. Nor had there been any indication she was romantically involved with another man. She was an attractive, intelligent woman of good character. Max figured he hadn't anything to lose by tendering his proposal.

Late one Friday afternoon, just after the first of the year, he had invited her to his office and in a businesslike manner had outlined the arrangement he had in mind. He had made it clear he wasn't in love with her, and since he didn't intend for them to have any children, he wouldn't force himself on her sexually. What he wanted, needed, was her companionship.

By the time he'd finished stating his case, Max had been sure she would refuse him. The shocked look on her face had made him realize just how egocentric he must have sounded. He was asking a lot, and in return, what he had to offer amounted to little more than financial security.

Max could guarantee that as his wife, Jane would never want for anything material. And if, for any reason, one of them wanted to divorce, he would see that she had a generous settlement. But Jane seemed perfectly capable of taking care of herself. With her background and experience, she could have her choice of high-paying jobs.

Yet Jane hadn't turned him down flat. Instead, she had calmly, quietly, met his gaze for what seemed like a very long time, then said she would like to think about it. Forty-eight hours later, sitting across from him again, she had accepted his offer of marriage with a composure that he had found deeply gratifying.

During the three months of their engagement, Max had found himself growing more and more pleased with her. She had seemed to understand exactly what he wanted of her, as well as what he had to offer her in return. Not love, but friendship. A warm, close friendship that he now realized could also include... sex.

He was physically attracted to her. Had been for weeks. But he hadn't allowed himself to acknowledge it until he'd kissed her at the chapel. He hadn't been able to deny it after that. Nor had he been left to wonder if the feeling was mutual. Not after the way she had kissed him back.

As Max drew closer to the open doorway leading out to the balcony, he recalled all the softly spoken words and casual touches, the smiles, the understanding, often sympathetic looks they had exchanged since they'd become a couple, and wondered why he hadn't realized much sooner that their compatibility could be physical, as well as emotional.

You didn't have to love someone to enjoy having sex with them. Some men didn't even have to like or respect a woman. Of course, Max wasn't one of *them*. Love might be out of the question, but for him, consummating his marriage without some fond feelings for his wife would have been impossible.

Luckily for him, at that moment his feelings for his wife just happened to be very fond, indeed.

Jane didn't look at him, nor did she speak as he joined her on the balcony. Only the slightest tensing of her slim shoulders indicated her awareness of his presence.

Max wondered if she might be afraid of him, then dismissed such a notion as nonsensical. He had never done anything to cause her, or any woman, to fear him, and he wasn't about to start now.

"Enjoying the view?" he asked, for want of a better opening.

"Oh, yes, it's lovely up here." She glanced at him, smiled slightly and seemed to relax. Lifting her face to the breeze that ruffled her dark curls, she added, "The sky is so clear, you can see for miles."

"An experience to savor, considering how often we're fogged in," he said as he loosened the knot of his pale gray silk tie.

"Before I came here to live, I never really believed the weather in Seattle could be as dreary as everyone claimed."

"And now?"

"Now I'm definitely a believer," she admitted with a hint of laughter.

"The good days—and nights—are *really* good, though."

"And we appreciate them that much more."

"Yes, we do, don't we?" Removing his tie, he stuffed it into the pocket of his dark gray suit coat, then unfastened the first few buttons of his white linen dress shirt. "Have a nice time tonight?" he continued, keeping his tone light.

"A very nice time." Finally, she turned to face him, her features shadowed in the darkness. "Thank you, Max. For making tonight...special."

"My pleasure," he replied, his gaze snagging on the lush curve of her mouth as he brushed a wisp of hair away from her face.

She had deserved more than a clandestine trip to the local justice of the peace, and luckily, he'd had sense enough to know it.

"Well, I suppose I should see if Calvin needs my help," she murmured as she took a step back.

"I told him to send the caterer's staff home and gave him the rest of the evening off."

"Oh..."

"I thought it was time I had you all to myself." Reaching out, he traced the line of her jaw with one fingertip.

"You did?" Her eyes wide, she glanced at him in obvious confusion.

"Mmm, yes, I did...."

Impatient as he was to have her, Max drew back. He had to give her a little time to adjust to his sudden change of heart. He was astonished by it himself. He could only imagine how she must be feeling.

"Why?" she asked, then looked away as if embarrassed by her temerity.

Most husbands would want their wives to themselves on their wedding night. But up until a few moments ago, Max had given every indication that was the *one* thing he wouldn't be wanting from her.

"For two reasons," he replied, still trying hard to maintain a lighthearted tone. "Come inside, and I'll explain. All right?"

"All right," she agreed, once again meeting his gaze.

With what he hoped was a reassuring smile, he took her hand in his and led her into the living room. He paused to close the balcony door, then turned to her again.

He had left only one lamp burning near the doorway that opened into the hall off which the bedroom suites were located. His and hers, though he hoped she wouldn't feel the need for separate quarters tonight—or any night—once he explained how his feelings for her had changed.

"First, I have something for you. Something I wanted to give you in private. A token of my... esteem."

He slipped a hand into his suit coat and took the long, flat black velvet box from the inside breast pocket. He held it out to her, but she didn't take it. Instead, she eyed it uncertainly for several seconds.

"Max, I don't think—" she began at last.

"Sometimes that's wise," he cut in teasingly. "Don't think, just enjoy."

She seemed about to argue, then gave in graciously.

"Well, if you insist."

"I do."

With a shy smile, she took the box from him and opened it. For several moments, she stared at the fragile gold bracelet set with row upon row of brilliant baguette-cut diamonds.

''Oh, Max…'' she whispered, blinking rapidly as if trying to hold back tears.

Touched by her obvious pleasure, he lifted the bracelet from the box.

''Here, let me,'' he muttered, his voice gruff.

Willingly, she raised her left arm. As she did so, the light glinted off the simple, unadorned gold wedding band she now wore on her ring finger. He pushed back the lace-edged sleeve of her dress, then clasped the bracelet around her wrist.

''It's lovely, Max, just lovely. Thank you.''

''You're welcome.''

Turning her hand palm up, he bent and pressed a kiss against the inside of her wrist. The faint scent of flowers and spice filled his senses as her pulse fluttered under his tender caress. When he raised his head, he saw her looking at him, her bright blue eyes filled with the same longing he had seen in them at the chapel.

Yes, he thought, *yes*. He had been right. She wanted more, too. More than the companionship he had thought would be all he'd have to offer her. Theirs might not be a love match, but that didn't rule out sex. Not when they were so obviously drawn to each other.

Allowing the barest hint of a satisfied smile to tug at the corners of his mouth, Max put his hands on his wife's shoulders and drew her closer. For one long moment, she seemed to resist, her body tensing at his touch as something vaguely akin to fear flashed in her eyes.

Max was too intent on his own wants, his own needs, to pay any heed to what was probably nothing more than shyness on her part. Had she pushed him away, had she said, "No, please don't," he would have released her in an instant. But she hadn't.

Bending his head, he brushed his lips over hers. Her breath caught for an instant. Then, with a soft sigh, she put her arms around his waist, tipped her face up and relaxed.

Goaded by the subtle invitation her actions seemed to offer, Max tightened his hold on her. Deepening his kiss, he nipped at her bottom lip with his teeth, then gently soothed with the tip of his tongue.

Again, Jane seemed to tense, her fingers clenching the fabric of his suit coat. Smoothing a hand down her back, Max cupped her bottom and pressed into her gently, showing her exactly what she was doing to him.

With a low moan, Jane parted her lips once more, granting him the access he desired. Pressing his advantage, Max took possession of her mouth, tasting her with the greediness of a man who had denied himself the comfort of a woman far too long.

He didn't want to stop kissing her. He wanted to go on and on, his tongue dancing over hers, binding her to him with a soul-searing intimacy as he tore the clothes from her body, freed himself, shoved her up against the wall and—

Shaken by the vividness, and the aggression, of the images in his mind, Max raised his head and took a step back. Not here, and not like that, he warned himself.

She was his wife. He owed her so much more than that. Owed her warmth, tenderness, affection. And he would try to give her all that, he vowed, meeting her glassy-eyed gaze.

Though how he would manage to restrain the wild,

fierce passion throbbing through him long enough to do so, he had no idea at all.

"Max, are you sure you want to...? That we should...?" she stammered, her voice shaky.

In her own cautious way, she was reminding him of their original agreement. A reminder he would heed if he had any sense at all, he acknowledged somewhere in the back of his mind.

But truly rational thought where Jane Elliott Hamilton was concerned had begun to fade with the first glass of champagne he'd drunk, then abandoned him altogether in the midst of that last kiss.

Well, not quite altogether. He was still sane enough to know she deserved one last chance to cut and run.

"You're free to go to your suite if you want," he said, releasing his hold on her.

"And if I don't?" she asked, standing her ground as she looked up at him.

"Then I'm taking you to bed," he stated, his tone matter-of-fact.

She didn't move. Not an inch. Just stood where she was and held his gaze.

With a growl of masculine satisfaction, Max closed what little distance remained between them, scooped her into his arms and headed toward the darkened hallway. His body thrummed with a desire so hot, so deep, so wild, that any lingering sense of caution faded into nothingness.

Jane Elliott Hamilton was his lawfully wedded wife. Tonight, he was going to avail himself of that fact, and the consequences be damned.

Chapter Two

With a tremulous sigh, Jane wrapped her arms around her husband's neck and nestled her head against his shoulder as he strode purposefully down the hallway. Hesitating not at all, he passed the doorway to her suite of rooms. He had meant what he'd said. He was taking her to bed. *His* bed.

She could have stopped him. He had given her the opportunity. In fact, she still could. As eager as Max seemed to have sex with her, saying the simple words ''No, don't'' would certainly end this…madness. Were she to insist, Maxwell Hamilton would honor their original agreement.

Yet Jane said nothing at all to dissuade him. Though she had every reason to do so. Or had thought that she did until the moment he'd kissed her in the chapel.

She had agreed to Max's marriage proposal because he had expressly stated that neither sex nor children would be a part of the bargain. Three months ago, those terms had suited her just fine.

By agreeing to become his wife, she knew she would be gaining not only the kind of security she had craved since her parents were killed when she was ten years old, but the companionship of a man she trusted, as well. A man who wouldn't expect her to service him sexually or bear his children—the two things she had vowed never to do after the horrifying experience she'd had in her first foster home.

Though she had never been raped, she had endured many other forms of sexual molestation at the hands of a man considered to be a pillar of the community over the three years she had lived in his house. Luckily, the man's wife had caught him at it just after Jane's thirteenth birthday, and blaming *her,* had Jane removed by social services.

By then, however, Jane's fear of any man trying to control her physically had been deeply ingrained, and she had lost any desire she might have had to marry or have children of her own. Not only had she learned a distaste for sex; she had also come to realize just how vulnerable a child could be without the protection of loving, caring parents. The risk that a child she brought into the world might end up as she had was one she had no intention of ever taking.

Considering how loathsome her limited sexual experiences had been, she should be terrified of what lay ahead once Max reached his bedroom. Oddly enough, she wasn't. A little fearful, perhaps. A little confused and uncertain, but not run-screaming-into-the-night frightened. Not of Max.

If she had learned anything over the past few

months about the man who held her in his arms, it was that he would never intentionally cause her any harm.

Long before Max had approached her with his totally unexpected offer of marriage, Jane had realized what a truly fine man he was. He had taken the small company he'd inherited from his father and built it into an internationally known corporation. But unlike many powerful executives, he had never stopped appreciating the hard work and loyalty of the people he employed. He could drive a hard bargain, and he didn't suffer fools quietly. He was a fair man, however. A man who believed in rewarding hard work and initiative.

Despite his reserve, or perhaps because of it, Jane had found it easier to work with Max than with any other man she had ever met. And during the three months of their engagement, serving as his hostess and attending social events with him, she had also found herself able to relax in his presence. To her surprise, she had even begun to enjoy the occasional touch of his hand on hers, the possessive slide of his arm around her waist and the brush of his lips on her cheek.

Gradually, the repulsive memories of an overweight, balding, stinking, sweating man rubbing up against her, pawing at her breasts or her buttocks, faded away. In their place, increasingly vivid imaginings of what it would be like to make love with Maxwell Hamilton lingered in her mind.

Jane had never thought she would find out. At least not until he kissed her at the chapel. Really *kissed* her in a way that all but curled her toes. Then she had begun to wonder if his feelings for her had changed over the course of their engagement, as well.

Love had certainly caught *her* unawares. Maybe he, too, had been hit by Cupid's arrow.

Just in case, she had fortified herself with several glasses of champagne during the reception. And once the last of their guests had left, she had chased away all thoughts that she was setting herself up for what could prove to be a major disappointment. Then she had gone to wait for him on the balcony.

Now it seemed that she hadn't. At least, not so far, she acknowledged as Max carried her into his bedroom and proceeded toward the huge bed—set in a curve of floor-to-ceiling windows—that shimmered in the star-shine and moonlight.

That her husband so obviously wanted to make her his wife in every way sent her spirits soaring. Their union wasn't going to be loveless, after all. And that opened a whole world of possibilities for them. Possibilities Jane had resigned herself to never having. Possibilities for all sorts of happily-ever-afters...

"I can lower the blinds on the windows if you'd prefer," Max offered as he set her on the bed.

"Only if you do," she replied, her voice quavering. "I like the moonlight."

"Me, too."

With a shy smile, Jane glanced up at him. Standing over her, surrounded by shadows that emphasized the hard line of his jaw and the high planes of his cheekbones, his neatly trimmed black hair now slightly mussed by the breeze on the balcony, he appeared rather fearsome. But it was the hot flash of desire she saw in his pale gray eyes that sent a tiny shiver stealing up her spine.

Quickly, she looked away again, unsure what to say or do next.

She had never been with a man in such an intimate setting. Nor had she ever expected to be. And while she had some knowledge of what she considered the basic mechanics of sex, she had never, ever, made love. She hadn't wanted to. But here with Max, the longing she felt to be held, to be kissed, to be touched with the tenderness he had always shown her was almost more than she could bear.

How could she let him know that without making a fool of herself? Or worse, putting him off.

Fiddling with the extravagant gold-and-diamond bracelet, now weighing warm and heavy against her wrist, Jane drew a breath and waited. She would have to trust Max to lead the way. As she did, with all her heart and soul.

"Nervous?" he asked, seeming to read her mind as he sat beside her on the bed.

Sliding an arm around her shoulders, he drew her close to his side.

"Just a little," she admitted, her voice barely above a whisper, then smiled as she realized what an understatement she had made.

Had she been in this situation with anyone but Max, she would have been hyperventilating by now.

"I won't hurt you," he stated as he brushed his lips against her temple.

"I know."

Shifting slightly, she curled against him, put her arms around his waist and closed her eyes. For several moments, she savored the warmth he offered her as she grew accustomed to the feel of his body. Despite the layers of clothing they wore, he radiated a strength, a solidity, that heightened her awareness of her own softer, gentler curves.

As a means of self-preservation, she had denied her womanliness for years. Now, secure in her husband's embrace, she delighted in it. She had chosen to be there with him. Chosen of her own free will. She wasn't helpless. Not with Max. Had never been— would never be. His passion for her, a passion edged with tenderness, made her indomitable.

When he reached out and cupped her cheek in his palm, she looked up at him, smiling with a confidence that—only momentarily—took her by surprise. She might not know much about making love to a man, but instinct would stand her in good stead. All she had to do was trust herself, as well as Max. Then any words she spoke, any moves she made, would be the right ones.

"You are so lovely," Max muttered, his breath warm against her brow as he bent his head. "So very lovely…"

The gawky girl she had once been wanted to deny it, but the admiration in his eyes stilled her tongue. Holding her gaze, he drew her closer, tangled his hand in her hair and kissed her.

He took his time with her, seeming to take as much pleasure as she in the start of their sensual, sexual journey. Neither of them had intended for this to happen. Yet neither of them resisted the swell of wanting, *needing,* that swept away every preconceived notion they'd had about the kind of marriage they would have.

As if sensing just how inexperienced she was, Max moved at a leisurely pace, giving her the time she needed to adjust to the feel of his hands and mouth on her breasts and belly, and when he had undressed her, as well as himself, the tender probe of his fingers, then his tongue between her legs.

His earthy sensuality banished any lingering shyness or hesitation on her part. Unable to deny him anything, she reveled in each new sensation, laying herself open to him with shameless abandon as the moonlight glinted off their sweat-soaked bodies. She couldn't seem to get enough of him. She kept wanting more…and more.

When he had her writhing and moaning beneath him, Max moved over her with an urgency that finally matched her own. He braced himself above her on his forearms and threaded his fingers through her tangled hair.

"Jane…?" he muttered, his voice ragged.

Just her name, nothing more, spoken with the slightest hint of question.

"Yes, Max, yes," she answered, lifting her hips to welcome him.

Unsuspecting, he drove into her, then went utterly still as she gasped at the pain he'd caused her. Rearing back, he stared at her, his brow furrowed.

"What the hell…?" he began. Then, as realization dawned, he smoothed the damp hair away from her face and feathered a kiss over her lips as he started to ease out of her. "God, Jane, I'm sorry. Truly sorry. I never thought—"

"I'm all right," she hastened to assure him.

Holding on to him, she willed herself to relax, and almost immediately, her body began to accommodate the breadth and depth of his penetration. As she thought of how intimately they were joined, threads of the pleasure he'd given her earlier returned, chasing away the lingering ache.

"Are you sure?" he demanded, a worried look in his eyes.

"Very sure." Smiling up at him, she shifted her hips, drawing him into her even more deeply.

Needing no other encouragement, Max let go of his control, not only taking all that she had to offer him, but giving to her in return until the pleasure of her release had her crying his name.

"Max, oh, Max..."

Closing her eyes, she clung to him as he slid an arm under her hips, arched his back and with a low moan, sought, then found his own release.

Moments later, he rolled to his side. Though he eased his weight off her, he seemed as unwilling as she to give up their newfound intimacy.

Jane didn't mind at all. She loved the feel of him deep inside her. Loved the sense of finally belonging to someone. Someone she trusted. Someone she——

"You should have told me you'd never had sex," Max said after a while. "If I'd known, I wouldn't have been so rough with you."

"But you weren't," she replied, rubbing her cheek against his chest.

"You may change your mind by morning."

"I won't."

"You're going to be sore."

"Well, I promise not to blame you," she assured him, a hint of laughter in her voice. "After all, I *was* a willing participant."

"That is true," he agreed.

Obviously satisfied that she bore him no hard feelings, he hugged her close for a moment, then yawned mightily and finally slipped out of her. Reaching down, he grabbed the blankets they'd kicked aside earlier and pulled them up. As he lay back again, he put an arm around her rather absently and closed his eyes.

Jane snuggled against his chest, waiting for him to say something more. So much had happened since he'd kissed her in the chapel. So much had changed between them. She wanted to know how he felt about it. And she wanted him to know how she felt, as well. But several minutes passed, the silence broken only by Max's steady breathing.

Eventually, Jane realized he had fallen asleep. Feeling oddly bereft, she murmured softly, "I love you, Max. Love you." They would have time enough to talk in the morning, she told herself as she eased away from him.

Yet, try as she might, Jane couldn't quite convince herself that words spoken between them in the light of a new day would be quite the same as words spoken in the magic of their moonlit night. Already she sensed the enchantment fading.

Beside her, Max shifted, then rolled toward her, looping an arm around her waist.

"Janie," he muttered, pulling her close again.

"Mmm, I'm here."

"Good…"

Smiling at how he'd turned her rather plain name into an endearment, Jane curled up against her husband and closed her eyes.

Nothing would change in the morning, she assured herself. Nothing could. Not when they loved each other as they surely did.

Chapter Three

Max knew where he was at once, though it was a place in a time to which he hadn't traveled for quite a while. He didn't want to be there. Didn't want to be in that busy, brightly lit delivery room, standing off to one side, heart pounding, the sweat streaming down his face mingling with the helpless tears burning his eyes and blurring his vision.

Yet he couldn't seem to move. He could only stand and watch as the others, the gowned and masked professionals, worked frantically to save the woman lying on the table. For the baby, time had already run out.

He saw her looking at him, her eyes glazed, her lips moving, and heard her words, slurred but still understandable.

"Help me, Max, please, help me...."

More than anything in the world, he wished that he could. But how? He hadn't the knowledge or the training necessary. He could only hover on the sidelines, ineffectual and afraid. So very afraid for the woman he loved.

There was something not quite right about her, though. Something that made the dream a little different.

The woman lying just beyond his reach, begging for his help, wasn't Alyssa. She was—

A jolt of panic zinged through Max. A jolt so powerful he came awake breathing hard, as if he had run for miles.

Jane...

This time, the woman in his dream hadn't been Alyssa, Max thought, staring at the ceiling. The woman had been Jane. But his panic, his despair, had been just as soul shattering.

Willing himself to calm down, he took several long, slow, deep breaths as the fine sheen of perspiration on his face, neck and chest began to dry.

Why on earth had Jane taken his first wife's place in that awful dream? He had made sure his relationship with her would not be anything like his relationship with Alyssa. He had built a wall around his battered, broken heart, locking away his emotions. So what could have possibly triggered...?

Oh, no, Max. You didn't do what I think you did....

Slowly, carefully, he turned his head and saw Jane lying no more than a foot from him in the massive bed, sleeping soundly. She was curled on her side under the covers, her back to him, her dark hair spreading in a silky tangle across the white linen pillowcase.

Gazing at her in the dawn light, Max gradually put together vague bits and pieces of memory until he had a fairly good idea of how the woman he'd married as a matter of convenience had ended up in the one place he hadn't thought he'd wanted her.

He had drunk more champagne than he should have, thus allowing his judgment to become impaired. Then he had acted in the kind of foolhardy manner one often lived to regret.

Just as he was now doing in *spades* for a multitude of reasons.

He knew he had told himself that having sex with Jane would be just that. The physical act of sex, meant to relieve…tension. Not lovemaking that also engaged the emotions.

But what had happened between them last night wasn't that simple. What had begun—in his mind, at least—as a seductive romp had quickly turned into something else altogether.

Despite her shyness, Jane had been so willing, so eager, that he had wanted to please her as much as himself. He had gotten so carried away, he hadn't thought about protection—a fact that now made him quail. Nor had he realized—until too late—that she was a virgin.

At first, he had been shocked. Then, aware that he was the only one who had ever reached that particular stage of intimacy with her, he had been thrilled. Acknowledging that she was his, *only* his, he had been filled with an odd sense of triumph as they'd mated. And afterward, holding her close, he had fallen asleep feeling utterly satisfied.

With the dawn of a new day and the return of his usual clearheadedness, however, Max found himself having some very serious second thoughts. As a means of self-preservation, he had gone into this marriage with no intention of falling in love, and he wasn't about to let one night of mad passion deflect him from what he still deemed the wisest course of action.

Granted, he would have to go back to his original plan. The one that included separate sleeping arrangements. Just living with Jane, not to mention working with her on a daily basis, was going to make it difficult enough for him to keep his hands off her. He couldn't have her in his bed, night after night, as well. That would only add fuel to the internal fire already smoldering deep inside him.

By putting as much distance between them as physically possible, he might just be able to stop thinking of her as anything more than a friend. Or at least that was what he hoped would happen.

As it was, he had barely enough fortitude to do so now. Just lying there, looking at her, he could hardly control himself. His whole body throbbed with the need to hold her close, to touch her, to kiss her, to tease and tantalize her until...

Drawing a sharp breath, Max clenched his hand. If he made love to Jane again, he would be opening himself up to a whole new world of heartache. He had been there. He had done that. And he had learned his lesson too well to tempt fate again.

Losing a friend, however dear, wasn't the same as losing someone to whom you'd given a piece of your soul. He had forgotten that last night, but he wouldn't forget again. He couldn't afford to. Not only for his sake, but also for Jane's.

In the heat of passion, he had changed the rules to suit himself. Luckily, it wasn't too late for them to get back on track. But once they were, he would have to make absolutely sure they never drifted off course again.

Jane was going to be confused enough as it was. But she was a sensible woman. She would understand. He would apologize, of course. A mistake had been made, and he was willing to own up to it. But surely no permanent damage had been done. And as long as he behaved himself in the future, he could see no reason why everything wouldn't work out as he had originally planned.

Aware that he had lingered long enough, and that he would rather not be in the bed, naked, when Jane awoke, Max eased away from her. Firm as the mattress was, it barely shifted under his weight. To his relief, Jane slept on, undisturbed.

Quickly, and as quietly as possible, he gathered up their rumpled clothing. His suit pants and jacket, her dress and silky undergarments he laid over the old-fashioned, navy blue wing-back chair. His shirt, underwear and socks he dumped into the laundry hamper in the bathroom.

Venturing back to the bedroom, he collected fresh clothes, thankful for the smooth, soundless glide of the dresser drawers, then headed for the shower, locking the bathroom door behind him to eliminate any chance of Jane walking in on him.

He stood under the hot spray as long as he dared, toweled off quickly, dressed in jeans and a white crew-neck sweater, then lathered his face with shaving cream. As he scraped his razor along one side of his face, he eyed himself in the mirror. He didn't much like what he saw.

Very shortly, he was going to say and do things that would quite possibly hurt his wife's feelings. But he didn't see that he had much choice. Try as he might, he couldn't think of any kinder, gentler way to extricate himself from his rather distressing predicament.

A few minutes later, teeth brushed and hair neatly combed, Max braced himself for the worst, unlocked the door and stepped into the bedroom.

Though Jane had shifted on the bed so that she now faced in his direction, she still seemed to be sound asleep. Max was relieved by the brief reprieve. He was also sorely tempted to leave her be.

He considered asking Calvin to explain his absence when she finally awoke, but then admitted that would be the coward's way out. *He* was the one who owed Jane some clarification of the situation. He was also the one who had to deliver it—no matter how uncomfortable that made him.

Max crossed the bedroom slowly, his footsteps muted by the thick pile of the wall-to-wall carpet. Absently, he noted that the day had dawned bright and clear. Though the bedroom windows faced west, and the light filtering through at such an early hour was still shadowy, the sky was definitely blue.

Perfect weather for the drive up the coast he'd decided to take, he thought without much enthusiasm. Had he been able to include Jane in the outing...

But he couldn't. As he had already acknowledged, he needed to put some distance between himself and his wife. Otherwise, he could end up compounding the mistake he'd made last night.

Reluctantly, Max sat on the edge of the mattress, his gaze drawn to Jane's face. She looked so young and vulnerable, lying alone in the big bed, cocooned in the white linen sheets, navy blue wool blanket and matching pin-striped comforter. And so damned desirable.

The urge to reach for her, to haul her into his arms and kiss her awake, shot through him. For the space of several heartbeats, he imagined what it would be like to tear off his clothes, crawl close to her womanly warmth and pick up where he'd left off the night before.

Much to his relief, a tiny seed of common sense lurking somewhere in the back of his mind held him still.

He had chosen to wed Jane Elliott because he wasn't madly, passionately in love with her, and equally important, never expected he would be. Now, faced with the possibility that he had presumed wrong, he had to patch up what he could of his so-called marriage of convenience. Otherwise, he was going to end up paying in a way that he simply couldn't afford.

As if sensing his presence, Jane opened her eyes. She blinked once, slowly, then again. Finally, looking highly confused, she met his gaze.

"Max?" she murmured, her voice husky.

"Mmm, yes," he responded.

Looking away for a moment, he shifted uncomfortably as he tried to decide how best to say what he felt he must without sounding like a fool, or worse, a callous, insensitive brute.

When he glanced back at her, she was still staring at him, obviously perplexed. But then a smile lit her eyes. He had thought she might be upset at finding herself in his bed, but she wasn't. Instead, she seemed quite pleased.

Something in his expression must have alerted her to his mood, however. Her smile vanished as quickly as it had appeared.

"Is something wrong?" she asked, clutching the blanket around her as she pushed up on one elbow.

"About last night..." He paused, cleared his throat, forced his gaze away from the enticing curve of her bare shoulders, then continued hurriedly. "I owe you an apology. I had no right to...seduce you the way I did. We had an agreement. One I had every intention of honoring. One I *will* honor in the future. But last night..." Again he paused, sighed, shook his head. "I drank too much champagne. That's no excuse, of course. But I really wasn't thinking straight. I'm sorry. Truly, I am. I swear it will never happen again."

She stared at him wordlessly, her lips slightly parted, a wounded look in her eyes. Suddenly, Max was afraid she might cry. What would he do then? What would he *say?* He didn't think he could hold firm against her tears. He would have much preferred recriminating words. He could have dealt with them so much more easily.

Hoping to avoid a scene, he stood quickly and moved away from the bed. Maybe tomorrow or the next day, they could discuss last night's aberrant behavior like the intelligent adults they were. By then, they would be able to put everything into proper perspective. For now, however...

"As I said, I'm sorry about what happened," Max repeated as he halted at the bedroom doorway. Facing her again, he studiously avoided meeting her gaze.

"Yes, I can see that you are," Jane stated simply, her chin tipped at a proud angle.

She had shifted into a sitting position, but still held the bedcovers tight around her.

"I wish I could make it up to you somehow...."

Increasingly unnerved by her composure, Max hesitated. Naked in his bed, her hair a tangled mess, she still managed to not only *look* every inch the proper lady, but to act like one, as well. Which made his own behavior seem even more execrable.

He didn't have to go on as he'd begun, he thought. He could stop now before any more damage had been done. He could go to her, he could bury his face in her lap and beg her to...

What? he wondered. Give him another chance to screw up the arrangement they'd agreed upon three months ago? The terms and conditions had suited him perfectly well then, and they would again, once he started thinking with his head.

"Maybe spending the day apart would be a good idea," he continued when she made no comment. He would have done almost anything she asked, but she seemed intent on holding her peace. Considering how untrustworthy he'd already proved himself to be, he couldn't really blame her. "That would give us a chance to step back, to reassess our...priorities."

"I'm sure it would," she agreed in a grave tone.

"Well, then, I'll leave you to get settled in your suite. Kerner will be available to lend whatever assistance you need." He started to turn away, stopped, looked back at her again. Feeling as if he were grasping at straws, he added, "Maybe the two of you could see to the wedding gifts, as well."

Surely sorting through the gaily wrapped packages they had received would give her some enjoyment.

"Yes, of course."

"I'll probably be gone until late tonight, so don't wait dinner for me."

"I won't."

Unable to think of anything more they needed to

discuss before he made a run for it, Max edged a little closer to the doorway. She knew that Kerner and the caterer's staff would handle whatever cleaning up was necessary. And they had already agreed that they would each continue to take separate cars to the office.

With equal parts relief and remorse, he realized that he wouldn't have to see her again until the staff meeting at ten o'clock tomorrow morning. Oh, he could always think of a good reason if he really wanted to. But he wouldn't. The time apart would do them both good. And by the next day, when they were both back to normal, they could resume cordial relations once again.

"I guess I'll be on my way, then." Against his better judgment, Max met his wife's gaze, then quickly turned away, the reproach he'd seen in her eyes grabbing at his gut.

"Have a nice day," she murmured.

"Yeah, you, too."

His heart unaccountably heavy, Max strode out of the bedroom without a backward glance. He knew that what he was doing was best. But he didn't feel good about it. Not at all.

In the kitchen, he found Calvin at the counter, pouring hot coffee into a china cup.

"Not only up, but already dressed, Max? Somehow, I thought you and Jane wouldn't stir outside your bedroom till well past noon," the butler teased, a twinkle in his eyes.

"Well, obviously you thought wrong," Max retorted rudely.

He rarely spoke to anyone in such a sour tone, and never to the dapper little man he now considered family. But he couldn't hide how his shame over the way he'd treated Jane had colored his mood.

"Obviously." Calvin eyed him narrowly for a long moment, then continued more formally. "Shall I fix a tray for the two of you, sir? Breakfast in bed, perhaps?"

"No, thanks."

Crossing the kitchen, Max opened a cabinet, retrieved a travel mug and moved to the coffeemaker. He filled the mug with coffee and snapped the lid in place.

"What the hell are you doing, Max?" Calvin asked, abandoning the role of manservant as quickly as he'd assumed it.

"Not that it's any of your business, *Kerner,* but I'm going out."

"Out? Alone?"

"Yes, *alone.*"

"But what about Jane?"

"Unless she decides otherwise, Mrs. Hamilton will be spending the day here, getting settled in her suite and sorting through the wedding gifts. I told her you would give her whatever assistance she needs."

"You know, Max, I had serious reservations about your...marriage. You could have hired a professional hostess to handle your social obligations. But when I saw the way you looked at Jane last night, I thought maybe you knew what you were doing after all. I thought maybe you had found what you've been missing since you lost Alyssa and the baby.

"Now I'm wondering what kind of cruel game you're playing. And I'm wondering why you chose to involve that lovely young woman. After all the years we've been together, I would have never thought you'd behave so...so—"

"Badly?" Max interjected sardonically.

"Yes."

"Sorry to disillusion you, but I guess that's the way it goes sometimes."

"I certainly hope not, sir. Not so much for your sake, but for Jane's."

Stung by the older man's harsh words, Max turned and headed for the hallway. He had always considered Calvin Kerner one of his closest allies. Now it seemed he'd changed allegiance, but in a perverse way, Max was glad.

With someone as loyal and true as Calvin Kerner looking out for Jane's well-being, he could rest easy. Until they were able to be friends again, she would be fine. Just fine and dandy.

"I'll be out late," Max advised.

"Shall I wait up for you?"

"Not tonight."

"Very good, sir."

Mug in hand, Max left the kitchen, stalked to the coat closet, grabbed his black leather bomber jacket and let himself out of the apartment. He took the elevator down to the parking garage, where he climbed into the sportier of his two cars, an expensive German import with a convertible top.

With the sun up and the sky clear, he headed for the highway that would take him north of the city. That early on a Sunday morning, he shouldn't have any trouble catching the ferry to Orcas Island.

He had always found the trip there enjoyable. There was no reason why he shouldn't do the same today.

No reason at all.

Chapter Four

Jane huddled beneath the tangle of sheets and blankets on Max's bed, the muffled snick of the door closing echoing in her ears long after he walked out on her.

At first, she had wanted to lay her head down and cry, but she had learned almost twenty years ago that tears did no good at all. The hurt wouldn't magically disappear. Dashed hopes and dreams wouldn't be restored. Especially hopes and dreams she had been a fool to entertain in the first place.

Last night, she had known that Max wasn't quite himself—that he wasn't exactly thinking straight. But instead of acknowledging that his sudden desire for sex was more alcohol induced than anything, she had chosen to believe he was in love with her.

She should have known better. Love had never been part of the *bargain* he'd offered her. He had made that completely clear from the start. And he hadn't said or done anything last night to give her good reason to think he'd changed his mind.

He had wanted sex, as any healthy, red-blooded man would, and she had been available. He hadn't coerced her by any means. She had gone with him willingly, making up fairy tales all along the way.

Theirs would be a real marriage, after all, she'd thought. A marriage filled with love. And Max would be more than the kind but emotionally distant friend she had thought she wanted three months ago.

She'd had to depend on herself for so many years. Having someone to look to for comfort and support— someone who could ease the loneliness that had come as a result of her determination to remain self-sufficient, yet would make very few demands on her in return—had seemed like a godsend.

Jane hadn't counted on falling in love with Max. Not when the mere thought of physical intimacy made her shudder with distaste. But Max had been so different from any of the other men she'd known, personally or professionally.

He had been the one to set the parameters for their relationship, and he had stayed well within them during their courtship. He had been true to his word, never once taking advantage of her, and quite naturally, her trust in him had grown. She had been sure he wouldn't step beyond the boundaries he had set without a very good reason. One that involved his deepest emotions.

Or at least that's what she had told herself last night....

Of course, she knew better now. All Maxwell Hamilton had really felt was a salaciously self-satisfying urge for the kind of bump-and-tickle he could dismiss as a mistake first thing in the morning.

Too much champagne, he'd said. Really wasn't thinking. Never happen again.

As if he'd not only come to his senses, but had found her wanting in the process.

Granted, she had been lacking in experience. Yet he hadn't given the impression that he'd been disappointed. In fact, he had seemed quite…content when all had been said and done. So content that he had fallen asleep holding her in his arms, she reminded herself, anger at herself, as well as at Max, edging away some of her pain.

Had she allowed her feelings for him to blind her to the possibility that he was just as capable as any man of using her for his own amusement? Was he really not all that different from her first foster father? Had he, too, taken advantage of her innocence?

Jane didn't want to think that of him. But how else could she explain his behavior over the past twelve hours? Not only had he apologized for seducing her, but he had also *seemed* truly sorry that he'd done it. Would he be experiencing such obvious regret if he'd been playing some sort of sordid game with her?

Too bad Max hadn't stuck around long enough for her to ask him. She would have liked to have had some answers. Unfortunately, stung by his plain speaking as she'd been, she hadn't been able to collect herself quickly enough. Holding back the tears prickling at the backs of her eyes while maintaining what dignity she could, sitting naked on his bed as he towered over her, grim-faced and aloof, had taken all her effort.

Amazingly, she hadn't been afraid of him—just hurt

and confused. As she still was, and would probably continue to be for quite some time.

But she was also pragmatic enough to know her options were limited. She could divorce Max, give up her job at Hamilton Enterprises and try to make a new life for herself elsewhere. Or she could take up her role as Max's wife in name only, and put last night behind her.

By making the latter choice, she wouldn't be doing anything she hadn't already agreed to. Only her expectations would have changed. And she had already admitted she shouldn't have had any of those where Max was concerned in the first place.

He had been honest about what he wanted from her, and that hadn't seemed to change. He had assured her he would honor their original agreement. What did she have to lose by giving him another chance? As long as *he* played by his rules from now on, she could, too. Couldn't she?

And if he wanted something more from her, something like last night?

Then he was going to have to prove to her that he wasn't acting on impulse again. Otherwise, she was going to keep him at arm's length.

Despite the way he had treated her that morning, she hadn't stopped loving him. Not completely. But she wasn't a masochist, either. She wasn't going to let him use her again just to gratify a sexual urge, no matter how he tried to charm her into it.

She had learned how to put the past behind her, make the best of present circumstances and continue to have hope for the future. She also knew better than to make the same mistake twice. She had allowed herself to be caught unawares only once while living in her first foster home. The same would hold true here. She would be on guard from now on. And she would survive as she always had—by making the best of things.

Feeling a little better, Jane sat back and took a look at her surroundings for the first time since she'd awakened. On previous visits to the penthouse, Max's private quarters hadn't been offered for her inspection. Now, as the light filtering through the windows that curved around the bed began to brighten, she could see that his bedroom was almost as impersonal as the rest of the apartment.

Though elegantly appointed with classic dark wood furniture and richly upholstered wing-back chairs, there wasn't much to distinguish it from an expensive hotel room. No framed photographs on the dresser, no magazines or books on the nightstands, no odds and ends from emptied pockets atop the chest of drawers.

Max had told her that he'd moved to the apartment seven years ago. Obviously, he had done so physically, but not emotionally. She couldn't say that she was surprised. A man who chose to have a wife in name only wasn't likely to have much interest in making a *home* for himself. Still, in a strange way, she was saddened for him.

He had offered only the barest of details about his past—that his first wife, Alyssa, had died, along with their baby.

He hadn't wanted to keep the house on Mercer Island, so he'd moved into the city.

Out of respect for him, Jane hadn't sought out more specific information. She hadn't really needed any. She was smart enough to put two and two together.

She had realized how much he must have loved Alyssa, and how devastated he'd been by her death.

So much that he never wanted to grow that close to a woman again.

Which made his behavior that morning even more puzzling, she thought. Unless his feelings for her had gone deeper than he'd intended.

Wouldn't he have been more jaded about taking her to bed if she didn't really matter to him? Jane couldn't say for sure because she didn't know him well enough.

More than likely, he'd been afraid she was having second thoughts about their marriage, and would leave him in the lurch. She had, of course. But not the kind that had probably concerned him.

Her first thoughts upon awakening had been wrapped in hazy ribbons of love and lifelong devotion. But Max must have assumed that separation and divorce were foremost on her mind. He had made what he'd considered a good deal. Then, in a moment of weakness, he had done something that could have ruined everything.

That was probably why he'd tossed apologies her way, then taken off as if he'd had the hounds of hell at his heels. Not because *she* mattered all that much to him, but because he had wanted to salvage what he could of their wedding venture.

He needn't have worried. She had agreed to marry him because she had believed that she would benefit from their union, too. And as long as he treated her with respect, there was a good chance that could still be possible.

Willing herself to look on the bright side, Jane glanced around Max's bedroom again. She was more than ready to put her wedding night behind her. But first she had to get back to her own room with as much grace as possible.

The thought of pulling on her wedding dress and scampering down the hallway like a criminal likely to be caught in the act made her cringe. Why try to hide what had happened between her and Max? Kerner probably knew already, and *she* certainly had no reason to be ashamed.

Might as well take a shower in Max's bathroom, wrap up in a borrowed bathrobe, collect her things and make a stately exit, she decided. No explanations or excuses were necessary, so why should she feel the need to offer them?

Rousing herself, Jane loosened her grip on the bedcovers. As she did, the gold-and-diamond bracelet Max had given her shifted on her wrist. She gazed at it with regret. An expensive piece of jewelry, lovely to look at, but certainly not the token of affection she had originally thought it to be.

Fumbling with the clasp, she managed to get it undone, then set it on the nightstand. Maybe she was being foolish, but she didn't want it. Not when it suddenly seemed like payment for services rendered.

She tossed the blankets aside and started to scoot toward the edge of the mattress. Immediately aware of the unfamiliar soreness coupled with an odd stickiness between her legs, she paused, glanced down and drew a quick breath.

There were dark, rusty smears on her upper thighs and also on the white linen sheets. Proof that she was no longer a virgin, she realized. And not something she wanted to leave behind for anyone to find.

Reasonably sure that nobody would bother her as long as the bedroom door was closed, Jane found a terry-cloth bathrobe hanging in Max's closet, then headed for the bathroom, where she took fresh towels from one of the cabinets. She was tempted to pamper herself with a long, leisurely bath in the huge marble tub, but settled for a shower instead.

She used Max's blow-dryer on her hair, finger combing it into a loose tangle of curls, then brushed her teeth with the new toothbrush she found in a drawer. After a few moments of searching, she came across fresh sheets in another of the cabinets, returned to the bedroom and changed the bed.

She gathered her dress, underwear and shoes along with the soiled linen, paused at the bedroom door, took several steadying breaths and finally stepped out into the hallway.

All was quiet in the apartment, but that was understandable. Even though it was still early, Kerner was probably up and about. But knowing Max, he'd probably asked the butler to give her some privacy. Part of her wanted to take all she could get. Yet she could only lay low for so long—especially with a bundle of Max's bed linens in her possession.

She stopped in her suite long enough to dress in gray wool slacks and a pale yellow sweater. She also took the time to put her things away. Then she headed resolutely for the laundry room she knew to be just off the kitchen.

As she passed through the living room, she noted that the only evidence left of the reception was the stack of gifts on the coffee table. Apparently, Kerner had quietly cleared away any other mess that had remained.

The butler—sitting at the kitchen table, a cup of steaming coffee at his elbow and the Sunday paper spread out before him—looked up at her in surprise, eyed the sheets she held in her arms, then stood.

"Mrs. Hamilton, there was no need for you—"

"I know, Kerner." She smiled brightly as she sailed past him. "Chalk it up to force of habit. I'm so used to straightening up after myself."

She continued into the laundry room without a backward glance. Though her hands trembled slightly, she managed to measure detergent into the washer and add the sheets and pillowcases. Deftly, she set the dials and started the machine before Kerner joined her.

"There...all done," she said, still smiling as she turned to face him.

"Mmm, yes." He met her gaze, his eyes filled with sympathy. "Now come and let me fix breakfast for you."

"Oh, I'm not really hungry," she protested.

"I thought maybe an omelet with fresh chives and grated cheese followed by a bowl of strawberries dolloped with double cream." He took her by the arm and gently steered her to a chair by the table. "Sit down while I get your juice and coffee."

"Well, if you insist," Jane acquiesced.

She loved nothing better than a hot breakfast, but rarely took the time to do more than pour dry cereal in a bowl and add milk. Taking Kerner up on his offer wouldn't cost her anything, and she certainly didn't want to hurt his feelings. He had been so kind to her in the weeks before the wedding.

"Just black, right?" he asked, setting a glass of orange juice and a mug of coffee on the table.

"Right." She offered him a slight smile. Then, turning her attention to the front page of the paper, she added as casually as she could, ''Did you see Max before he left?''

''He graced me with his presence for all of five minutes,'' the butler replied as he cracked eggs into a bowl.

''So you know he'll be gone until late tonight.''

''That's what he said, the damned fool.''

At Kerner's caustic comment, Jane looked up in surprise. The dapper man glanced at her, winked broadly and turned back to the stove.

''Running scared, I imagine,'' he said. ''But don't worry. He'll come to his senses eventually. Just be patient with him.''

''I will,'' Jane murmured, lowering her gaze, uncomfortable with the turn their conversation had taken.

She liked Calvin Kerner quite a bit. He had been a great help to her during her engagement to Max, coordinating schedules and assisting with dinner-party plans. He had always treated her with respect. He'd also made her feel like a welcome addition to the family.

But now he seemed to be going a step further, showing her the kind of allegiance she'd thought it would take years to earn. She wasn't sure what she'd done to deserve it. But knowing that she had it eased some of the embarrassment she'd been suffering as a result of Max's desertion.

Of course, she didn't want to come between her husband and his butler. Asking Kerner to choose sides was something she would never do. But she could see no reason why he couldn't look out for her best interests, as well as Max's, without doing Max a disservice.

Jane glanced through the paper, not really paying much attention, while Kerner finished preparing her breakfast. When he joined her at the table again, her omelet and strawberries in hand, she glanced up gratefully.

"Thank you, Kerner. Everything looks delicious."

"You're most welcome, Mrs. Hamilton."

"'Jane,'" she said, meeting his gaze again.

"'Calvin,'" he replied, nodding as if they'd just been introduced, a conspiratorial twinkle in his eyes.

She nodded, too, then dug into the fluffy omelet.

Calvin refilled her coffee cup, as well as his own, set the thermal carafe on the table and sat down across from her.

"The staff from the catering company will be here at one o'clock to collect the last of their things," he advised, gesturing to the neatly stacked boxes near the apartment's rear service door.

"You should have waited to finish the cleanup. I could have given you a hand."

"My job, not yours," he replied in a kindly tone.

"But I feel I should be doing something to help out around here."

"What with your job and the spring social season swinging into high gear, not to mention whipping that husband of yours into shape, you're going to have enough to keep you busy in the weeks ahead. Let me worry about running the household. Otherwise, I won't feel like I'm earning my keep."

"All right," Jane agreed, feeling her face grow hot.

She had about as much chance of whipping Maxwell Hamilton into shape as she did of flying to the moon. But there seemed no point in reminding Calvin of that fact. Obviously, he wanted to believe her marriage to Max could be a *real* marriage. What good would it do to belabor the fact that it never would?

"I trust you have everything you need in your suite?" Calvin continued.

"Yes, thank you."

She had been given free rein in decorating the bed-sitting room and adjoining bathroom to her taste. But aside from a fresh coat of paint and the addition of floral-print wallpaper in the bathroom, there hadn't been much to do. She had used some of her own furniture and put the rest in storage, staying in a nearby hotel the past few days so that her things could be in place by the weekend, making the transition relatively easy.

"Well, then, I suppose we had better get started on the wedding gifts."

Finishing the last of her strawberries, Jane agreed.

Foolishly, she had assumed Max would share that task with her. Since he'd chosen not to, she would just as soon get it out of the way as quickly as possible.

By the time the caterer's staff arrived, Jane and Calvin had completed the unwrapping, cataloging and storing away of the extravagant assortment of crystal and silver. She had lingered over only three of the gifts, all of which she'd taken to her room—the Waterford bowl from Emma, the sterling-silver frame from Megan and the porcelain candlesticks from Kathleen.

Though scattered far and wide, and for one reason or another unable to make the trip to Seattle, each of her closest friends had made a special effort to send her best wishes for Jane's happiness. Of course, they hadn't known any of the details. But why cause them any worry? They all had enough problems of their own.

Once the caterer's staff had departed, the remainder

of the afternoon and evening loomed depressingly. She thought about getting a start on the thank-you notes, but she wasn't in the mood. She also thought about going to the office for a while, then considered how embarrassing it would be if she ran into anyone there.

Bad enough to be going back to work tomorrow. She would rather do almost anything than risk being caught at the office today. She might be having one of the most dismal honeymoons on record, but the employees of Hamilton Enterprises didn't need to know that.

Although the sky had begun to cloud over, Jane finally decided a long walk to the Pike Street market would do her the most good. The physical exercise would ease the tension squeezing at the back of her neck, and being out among other people, watching them interact, would take her mind off her own problems.

She told Calvin not to bother with dinner—she could grab a bite to eat at one of the little cafés along the way. Then she headed out, umbrella in hand, gladly mingling with the others taking advantage of what had begun as a lovely day.

Only when she glimpsed a couple, walking hand in hand, did she think about Max, and then just for a moment or two. There was no use wishing for something she couldn't have. Not when she had been blessed in so many other ways.

Many hours later, Jane slipped into the apartment. Thanks to the rain that had been falling since early evening, she was cold and wet, as well as worn-out. Giving the kitchen and Calvin a wide berth, she went straight to her room, soaked in a hot bath, pulled on

a long plaid flannel nightgown and crawled into bed
with what she hoped would be a good book.

Long about midnight, she set aside the book, no
longer able to pretend it engaged her interest enough
to keep her mind from wandering. She switched off
the lamp and settled under the bedcovers, staring into
the darkness.

Her bed was also set in an arch of windows much
like the one in Max's bedroom. But tonight, a heavy
bank of clouds hid the moon, and rain tap-tapped
steadily against the glass. Most nights, the sound of it
would have soothed her to sleep. But she had too
much on her mind to rest so easily.

Was Max still out? she wondered. Considering the
turn the weather had taken, she hoped not. But there
was no way for her to know. To assure her privacy,
her suite was designed to be soundproof. With the
door closed, she wouldn't have heard him come in.
And she didn't dare creep into the hallway to take a
look around. Considering the kind of luck she'd had
lately, she would probably run smack into him and
have to explain what she was doing.

She shouldn't care about him. Not really. He was a
grown man, perfectly capable of looking after himself.
But she *did* care about him. Desperately…

Jane had no idea when she finally fell asleep, but
the sound of her alarm going off at six o'clock came
much sooner than she would have liked. At least she
had somewhere to go and something to do. Something
that would keep her mind fully occupied for the major
part of the day.

She washed and dressed quickly, choosing one of
her classically tailored black wool suits and a pale
peach silk blouse. With her hair scraped into a knot at

the nape of her neck and the barest hint of makeup, she looked like herself again. She added pearl earrings and the gold watch she'd bought to celebrate her promotion, and was ready to go.

She crossed to the desk, collected her briefcase, purse and car keys, then strode purposefully to the door. She wasn't sure about Max's early-morning routine. But she certainly didn't want to run the risk of having to sit across the table from him while Calvin fussed over their breakfast. Better to stop for coffee and a roll at the deli on the ground floor of the office building, she decided.

Schooling herself not to glance up the hallway toward Max's bedroom, Jane headed toward the living room, moving as quietly as she could.

"You're up early."

Startled by the sound of Max's voice close behind her, Jane gave a little cry as she stumbled over her own feet. Reaching out, Max caught her by the arm, steadying her, then quickly let her go again.

Glancing up at him, she forced herself to smile politely.

"So are you," she acknowledged, not quite meeting his gaze as he hovered over her in the dimly lit hallway.

He was dressed in suit pants and a dress shirt, but much to her relief, his feet were bare and he hadn't shaved yet. She had the head start she'd hoped for, and meant to use it to her advantage.

"Any special reason?" he asked.

"That report on the service problems we've been having with the T-300 series," she replied, thinking quickly. "I was hoping to have a chance to look over it before the staff meeting."

Actually, she had done that Friday afternoon, but it wouldn't hurt to refresh her memory.

"Your team worked fast."

"Yes, they did," she agreed, almost adding that he would be pleased with the results. Luckily, she caught herself just in time. "Now I have to do my part, so I'd better be off."

Smiling apologetically, she turned away.

"Jane…wait."

He took her arm again, halting her in midstep.

Something in his tone had her bracing herself. For what, she did not know. But obviously, he had sought her out for a specific reason.

"Yes?" Again, she faced him, this time tipping her chin up and looking at him eye to eye.

"You left this on my nightstand."

He held out a hand, the gold-and-diamond bracelet dangling from his long, lean fingers.

She could have taken it from him, pretending she'd forgotten it. But she couldn't be that dishonest.

"Yes, I know," she stated simply.

"But it's yours. I wanted you to have it," he insisted, unable to hide his confusion.

"I know that, too. However, I don't feel right about accepting it."

"I don't understand. The other night—"

"The other night was a mistake," she interrupted, her voice firm. "You said so yourself, didn't you?"

"Well, yes, but—"

"And I have to agree," she cut in again. "A mistake was made. One I'd rather not be reminded of. Surely you can see that, can't you?"

Giving him no chance to respond, Jane swung away from him and hurried down the hallway. To her relief, he didn't try to argue with her. Nor did he follow after her.

They didn't cross paths again until the staff meeting later that morning, and he treated her no differently than he had in the past. He was just as cool and aloof as always. But there was a look in his eyes whenever their gazes met that gave her pause.

Whatever it was, it couldn't be hurt. There was simply no way, she told herself. You had to care for someone deeply for him or her to be able to cause you pain.

And Maxwell Hamilton had made it perfectly clear that he never had, nor ever would, care for her that way.

Chapter Five

The party at the Four Seasons Hotel, hosted by Parker Campion, senior partner of Hamilton Enterprises's advertising agency, Campion-Dewitt, had been in full swing for well over an hour. Once again, Parker had gone all out on the annual soiree that was meant to be a way of showing appreciation to the many clients who had contributed to his success.

As had been the case with most of the social functions to which he had been invited in the past, Max had always dreaded attending, whether on his own or with a date. Not only had his bachelor status made him uncomfortable, but all too often, he'd also had to be downright rude about how best to end the evening—his place or hers—when all he'd really wanted was to be left alone.

With Jane by his side, he had thought such occasions would be more enjoyable. He had the ideal companion—a lovely wife, capable of holding her own among his associates, whose presence guaranteed that all but the most outrageously amoral would set their sights elsewhere. A wife who acted as a buffer whenever necessary, then faded quietly into the background, giving him all the solitude he wanted...and more.

Yes, indeed, Max acknowledged as he waited for the bartender to pour a double shot of bourbon on the rocks. He had the wife he'd thought he wanted, and what, for him, should have been the perfect marriage.

But in the ten weeks since his wedding, Max had slowly come to realize that what had seemed, in theory, like an ideal relationship was something else altogether when actually put into practice.

Not through any fault of Jane's. She had put herself at his beck and call twenty-four hours a day, seven days a week. And she had held up her end of the bargain impeccably, playing her role with a quiet dignity Max often found unnerving, not only in public, but in private, as well.

Yet she always seemed just beyond his reach. When she looked at him, she rarely met his gaze, and when she spoke to him, her voice was always matter-of-fact. While she never seemed cold and distant, she wasn't warm and friendly toward him, either. She rarely smiled when they were alone together, and she never laughed aloud. Granted, they hadn't shared all that many joyful moments, but their life together hadn't been deadly dull and dreary, either.

Had he treated her so badly that she felt she must always be on guard around him? He didn't like to think so. Yet that was how she seemed to be lately. Careful...very, very careful...not to let him get too close. And sometimes, at the oddest moments, she looked so...sad.

More times than Max could count, he had wanted to gather his wife into his arms and promise her everything would be all right. But he didn't dare. Not knowing, as he did, exactly where *that* would lead.

He would not think twice. Nor would he hesitate an instant. He would sweep her off her feet, carry her to his bedroom and toss her on the big, empty bed where he'd spent most nights tossing and turning alone since he'd been fool enough to declare that having sex with her had been a mistake he would never make again.

So many, many times in the past ten weeks, Max had wished he could take back those words. Or rather, had the courage to take them back. He hadn't thought he wanted the emotional commitment he'd been on the verge of making to her, so he'd tried to nip it in the bud. Tried and, obviously, failed.

But after such a cruel, heartless declaration, what could he say that wouldn't sound...self-serving?

Having sex with you wasn't a mistake, after all. In fact, having sex with you was really great. So great, I'd like to do it again and again and—

A sudden burst of laughter a little distance from where Max stood interrupted his reverie. Recognizing the lighter, more musical tone underlying the harsh guffaws, he looked up and saw his wife standing amid an admiring group of men, most of whom he didn't know.

A frown creasing his forehead, Max collected his drink. He swallowed a mouthful of the smoky bourbon, then eyed his wife critically.

He hadn't seen her quite so relaxed or so animated in months—two and a half months, to be exact. She certainly seemed to be enjoying herself, and she was obviously the center of her little circle's attention.

Understandable, Max admitted with an odd mix of gladness and dismay. He was gratified by her popularity. But seeing Parker Campion and Brett Dewitt, along with several strangers, hovering so close, eyeing her lasciviously, had him clenching his fists, ready to do battle. She was *his* wife, and suddenly, inexplicably, he had the most unholy urge to make sure everyone in the crowded ballroom knew it.

Another gulp of bourbon helped him maintain some semblance of self-control as he continued to gaze at her assessingly. She was so bright, so engagingly intelligent that she could talk to anyone about almost anything. And she was so damned lovely to look at.

Dressed in a simple black silk dress with a modestly high neck and a rakishly low-cut back, her hair twisted into a sophisticated French knot and her only jewelry the plain gold wedding band on her ring finger and a pair of pearl-drop earrings, she looked not only incredibly elegant, but also sexy as hell.

She seemed a little thinner than she had a few weeks ago, though. And, he noted, there were faint shadows under her eyes that her makeup couldn't quite hide.

With sudden concern, Max realized that lately Jane had seemed awfully tired, too. The long hours she spent at the office, coupled with a social calendar that most of his associates' nonworking wives found exhausting, had apparently begun to catch up with her.

Today was a perfect example. She had left for work before seven that morning, stopped at the apartment twelve hours later to shower and change clothes, then left again with him to attend Parker's party. If they stayed another hour or so, the requisite amount of time necessary to avoid seeming antisocial, they wouldn't get home until midnight or later. And tomorrow, Wednesday, she would be up early again, preparing for another busy day.

Knowing how much she loved her job, Max didn't feel right about asking her to limit the time she spent at the office. She seemed to enjoy being there so much more than she enjoyed being in the apartment. He couldn't say he blamed her. He hadn't intended for them to make a home together. She wasn't supposed to be that kind of wife. So why expect her to act as if she were?

At least she would have most evenings free for the next two weeks. He was leaving on a business trip to the Orient tomorrow afternoon, and had accepted invitations to only a couple of functions Jane had indicated she wouldn't mind attending on her own.

That would surely help to ease some of the strain she'd been under lately. But it wouldn't be the same as having a real vacation—something Max now realized she needed just as much as *he* did.

Just as soon as he got back to Seattle, he would broach the subject with her. A week or two, even three, at a lush resort on one of the more secluded Caribbean islands would do them both a world of good. And maybe spending some time alone together in a more relaxed atmosphere would cause some significant changes in their relationship.

He hadn't considered a honeymoon necessary when he'd planned their wedding. At that moment, however, he couldn't think of anything he wanted or needed more. Hell, they could stay away for a *month* if that was what it would take to get her to smile at him the way she was now smiling at Parker Campion.

Having stood by quietly as long as he could, Max swallowed the last of his drink, slammed the glass on a passing waiter's tray, then made his way to his wife's side. He didn't care if they were labeled antisocial. They were going to call it a night.

He would use his impending trip as an excuse and take Jane home to bed. Not *his* bed, of course. Not until they had a chance to talk. Really talk, soberly and sensibly, as they would be able to do off on their own, walking along a sandy beach under a balmy, starlit sky on Antigua or Martinique.

As if sensing his approach, Jane looked in his direction. She met his gaze for an instant, her smile wavering, then turned back to her companions. She seemed absorbed in whatever Brett Dewitt was saying, but as Max drew closer to her, he noted the slight stiffening of her shoulders that accompanied the second, warier glance she shot his way.

Max considered changing directions, seeking out someone else and initiating a conversation of his own so she could enjoy herself a little longer. But he had never been one to avoid the inevitable. Sooner or later, he and Jane would have to leave the party. And while she wouldn't be any happier to see him walking toward her an hour from now, there was a good chance she *would* be on the edge of exhaustion by then.

He should have realized long before now that she had been burning the candle at both ends. Unfortunately, he'd been too busy trying to think of a way to get her back into his bed without actually admitting he'd acted like a jerk to notice that she had run herself ragged attempting to fit the mold he'd cast for her.

But that was going to change. Just as soon as he returned from the Orient, they were going to make a fresh start. Though he'd given her every reason to, he didn't think she hated him yet. So they could still have a good life together, just the two of them, once they patched things up. A physically, as well as emotionally, fulfilling life together, he assured himself, recalling just how wantonly she had responded to him on their wedding night.

For a moment, Max savored the memory of Jane clinging to him, calling his name, then brought his thoughts back to the matter at hand. Right now, he would do best to concentrate on getting his wife home without causing her any upset. The rest would follow naturally.

Easing his way between Jane and Parker, Max slipped an arm around her shoulders. She tensed noticeably at his touch, and when she looked at him, her smile seemed much more forced than it had only a few minutes earlier. Filled with remorse, Max sighed inwardly. He really *had* made a mess of things.

"Ah, come to claim your wife, Hamilton?" Parker asked, grudgingly making a place for him in the group.

"Yes, I have."

"Sure you wouldn't rather discuss the latest in microchip technology with your old buddy Herb?" Parker teased. "He's over there at the buffet table."

"Positive," Max replied, then turned to Jane. "I know it's still early, darling. But if you don't mind, I'd like to head for home."

Jane's eyes widened almost imperceptibly at his use of the endearment, but she gave no other indication that he was acting out of character.

"I don't mind at all," she assured him as she met his gaze.

"Come on, Max. Don't be a party pooper. You and Janie just got here," Brett Dewitt protested.

Max swung toward Parker's young partner, his eyes narrowing suspiciously. *Janie?* To his knowledge, nobody ever called her that. Well, nobody but *him*, and then only that one time just after they'd—

"Max is leaving for two weeks in the Orient tomorrow," Jane explained. "And you haven't finished your packing yet, have you?"

"Er, no..."

Actually, Calvin always took care of that for him, but he saw no need to say so.

"Well, then, do whatever it is you have to do. But don't drag Jane along with you," Parker said. "Let her stay and have some fun."

"I've had a wonderful time. Really, I have." Jane reached out and touched Parker's sleeve in a gesture of gratitude, then added, "But I'm going home with my husband."

To Max's surprise, she slid an arm around his waist and leaned close to him, taking on the role of devoted wife so naturally that she had everyone in the group eyeing her indulgently.

"Hey, I forgot. You're still newlyweds." Parker grinned and winked at Max. "You two are going to be doing a hell of a lot more than packing suitcases tonight, aren't you?"

Bright spots of color bloomed on Jane's cheeks. Wordlessly, she ducked her head. Sensing her embarrassment, Max drew her more firmly into his embrace. Though Parker hadn't meant any harm, his sexual innuendo had obviously made her uncomfortable. And there was only so much pretending Max had a right to expect her to do.

"I always knew you were a smart man," he countered smoothly. "Now, if you *gentlemen* will excuse us…"

Keeping his arm around Jane's shoulders, Max guided her through the crowd, nodding and exchanging greetings without stopping along the way. Jane seemed content to stay close to his side. But once they were outside the ballroom, she glanced at him, smiled apologetically, then eased away from him.

Reluctantly, Max let her go. He knew as well as she that there was no need to continue their charade. To insist would only bewilder her all the more.

Until he had time to prove to her that his most recent change of heart wasn't just another whim, he didn't want to do anything that might alarm her.

"Nice party," he said as they crossed the hotel lobby.

"Yes, very nice," she agreed.

They walked to the front entrance, where Max gave the parking valet his ticket, then stood silently, waiting for his car to be brought around.

Looking at Jane out of the corner of his eye, Max noted again how tired she seemed to be. There was a barely noticeable slump to her shoulders, and her head dipped wearily as she stared blankly at the pavement beneath her feet. In the play of light and shadows under the canopy, her face appeared even paler and more drawn than it had earlier.

Unable to hide his concern, Max reached out and touched her cheek.

"Are you feeling all right?" he asked.

With a visible effort, Jane gathered herself together, met his gaze steadily and smiled.

"Of course. I'm feeling just fine."

Max knew that she was lying. How, he wasn't quite sure. But before he could press her further, his car rolled to a stop in the driveway and the valet hopped out.

They made the short drive to the apartment building in strained silence. He could ask all the probing questions he wanted, but if she chose to put him off—as she evidently did—she most certainly would.

They would both end up out of sorts, then he would be gone for two weeks. He certainly didn't want to leave her with angry thoughts or hurt feelings that could fester. Then she would never be amenable to the changes he hoped to make in their relationship.

He'd be better off talking to Calvin. The man doted on her. Surely, he would know whether she was having any problems with her health.

If Calvin suspected anything, he would cancel his trip, Max decided. If not, he would ask the butler to see to it that she got some rest while he was away.

At the apartment, Max thought of asking Jane to have a nightcap with him—something they had done occasionally after an evening out. But she looked so drained, he hadn't the heart to keep her up any later than necessary.

"Why don't you sleep in tomorrow morning?" he suggested instead. "Then we could have a late breakfast before I leave for the airport."

"I'd love to, Max. Really, I would," she replied. "But I have a nine-o'clock meeting in Tacoma with that new software-design group. I've already had to reschedule once. I'd hate to put them off again."

"I understand."

Much as he wanted to insist she do just that, he couldn't. He had no right to expect her to postpone a meeting at the last minute. Not when she had been working so hard over the past six months to add innovative products to Hamilton's growing line of software.

And she *had* sounded honestly regretful.

"Maybe I can get away early enough to see you off at the airport," she offered. "What time does your flight leave?"

"Twelve-thirty."

"Oh, right. Well, probably not." She shook her head ruefully. "I'm taking them out to lunch, too."

"No, probably not."

"Well, then, I suppose I'll see you when you get back. Two weeks, right?"

"Two weeks from tomorrow." He gazed at her steadily. "Clear your calendar."

She eyed him uncertainly for several moments, then nodded slowly.

"I will."

They wished each other a polite good-night, then Max stood alone in the dimly lit living room, watching as Jane disappeared down the hallway.

He wasn't ready to go to his room yet. Nor did he want to sit alone, drinking. A glance at his watch told him it was just ten o'clock. Thinking that Calvin rarely called it a night until after the late news, Max headed for the kitchen.

Sure enough, he found the butler in his sitting room, dressed in pajamas and a robe, slouched in his ratty recliner, using the remote control to switch channels on the big-screen TV that filled one wall.

"You're home early," Calvin commented, sparing him no more than a glance. "Party not up to Parker's usual standards?"

"The party was fine, but Jane seemed tired."

"Oh, really?"

Seeing that he now had Calvin's undivided attention, Max frowned as he added, "I'm worried about her. She looks like she's lost weight."

"Perhaps a little, but I'm sure she'll gain it back," Calvin murmured cryptically.

"Has she said anything to you about feeling ill?" Max pressed on.

"Not a word."

"Well, do *you* think there's something wrong with her? Physically, I mean."

"Nothing *wrong* at all, Max. Not that I can see."

"Maybe she's just run-down."

"Maybe…" Calvin agreed, though there was something vaguely sardonic in his tone.

Wondering if the man was being deliberately obtuse, Max made no effort to hide his irritation.

"Do you know something I don't?" he demanded.

"Only that on occasion you can be thicker than a plank."

"And what exactly is *that* supposed to mean?"

"If you treated your wife the way a husband should, you wouldn't be asking me about her well-being," Calvin replied quietly.

Stung by the truth of the man's simple statement, Max turned on his heel and stalked back across the kitchen. Halfway along, he paused, considered going back and demanding an understandable explanation, then thought better of it. Like Jane, Calvin had said all he intended to say on the subject.

Instead, Max called out loudly, "Did you finish my packing?"

"Of course, sir. All finished," Calvin shouted back,

enunciating each syllable in the falsely deferential tone he used to show displeasure.

"That was good of you."

"Not at all, sir. I'm paid to help make your life a little easier."

"Yeah, right," Max muttered.

Easy was the one thing his life *hadn't* been since his marriage to Jane. At least not in the way he had anticipated. And much as he hated to admit it, he had only himself to blame.

He hadn't factored in the possible repercussions that could result from a night of mad, passionate sex. Or rather, how he'd dealt with it the morning after. He had been so intent on avoiding emotional involvement that he'd behaved so badly, he had alienated the two people closest to him.

But only temporarily, he reminded himself. Once he returned from his trip abroad, he would set about righting the wrongs he had done Jane and, in his more defensive moments, Calvin, too.

Tonight, however, he would have to make do with his own less-than-splendid company. His lingering worry about Jane still eating at him, he stopped at the wet bar to pour a glass of brandy before going on to his bedroom.

Max wanted to believe Calvin would have told him if he suspected Jane was seriously ill. Yet the butler hadn't completely discounted his concern. Instead, he had been hinting at something. Something he seemed to think Max should be aware of. But *what?* No matter how he racked his brain, he hadn't a clue.

In the hallway, Max paused outside Jane's bedroom door. Closed, but not locked, he knew for a fact. But still a barrier he dared not breach.

Late one sleepless night, he had stood there, just as he was now. He had reached out, turned the knob and opened the door an inch or two. Then he had realized what he was about to do. Quickly, quietly, he had pulled the door shut and gone back to his room. Just as he knew he should do now.

Jane needed a good night's sleep more than she needed a confrontation with him. And it was definitely time to start putting her needs before his. They could sort things out just as easily in two weeks' time.

He had concentrated so long and so hard on how to avoid any kind of emotional entanglement that might cause him pain. He had lost sight of the fact that Jane had feelings, too.

Feelings he had been too afraid to encourage ten weeks ago when he'd seen her smiling at him sleepily amid the tangle of sheets and blankets on his bed.

Feelings he could only hope he hadn't crushed completely.

[faded text from previous page showing through]

Chapter Six

"Please, Ms. Elliott, have a seat," Dr. Marcus Four-neau invited, his smile warm and reassuring, as Jane halted hesitantly just inside his office doorway.

Too nervous to speak, she nodded, then moved awkwardly to one of the two upholstered chairs facing the wide mahogany desk where he stood. Behind her, the door to his private office closed with a muffled whoosh and click. Clutching her purse in both hands, she sank down gratefully and took several deep breaths, hoping to calm the wild beating of her heart.

This was it. The moment of truth. The results of the urine analysis and blood test she'd been given upon her arrival well over an hour ago were ready. The physical exam had been completed. Within a matter of moments, her suspicions would finally be confirmed or denied.

Jane had tried to ignore the signs and symptoms,

blaming the missed periods, the fatigue, even the bouts of nausea she had suffered intermittently on the stress caused by the recent changes in her way of life.

She had never had what could be called a regular monthly menstrual cycle, and the long hours she put in at the office, coupled with a busy social schedule, would have made anyone weary. The nausea, often accompanied by vomiting, had begun to frighten her, though. A touch of the flu, she'd told herself the first few days. But after almost three weeks, she hadn't been able to fool herself any longer. Either she was seriously ill, or—

"Don't look so frightened, Ms. Elliott," Dr. Fourneau chided kindly. "I can say with complete confidence that you're *not* suffering from any life-threatening disease. Aside from being slightly underweight, you're in excellent health."

"That's good," she murmured.

"Yes, very good indeed, considering you're also about ten weeks' pregnant."

"Pregnant." Jane said the word aloud without inflection.

A simple statement for a major complication she had spent the past few weeks refusing to consider.

Somewhere in the back of her mind, she had known it. But until now, she hadn't allowed herself to actually accept it. She had told herself that it couldn't have happened. That surely one night of lovemaking wouldn't result in a baby. So many women her age, desperate for a child, tried to conceive for years without success.

But she wasn't stupid. She and Max had had sexual intercourse, and neither of them had thought to use protection. There had been nothing to prevent his sperm from joining her egg, and obviously, nothing had.

"Yes, pregnant." The doctor beamed delightedly, then added, "Considering the date of your last menstrual period and the changes in your body I detected during the physical examination, I've calculated the baby's due date to be December 23. Just in time for Christmas, or New Year's at the latest."

A baby. Just in time for Christmas...

Overwhelmed by the increasing reality of what the very near future held in store for her, Jane closed her eyes and bowed her head. Instinctively, she pressed a hand over her belly protectively.

Not *a baby,* she amended. *Her baby.* And Max's...

"Are you all right, Ms. Elliott?" Dr. Fourneau asked as he touched her shoulder.

Looking up at him, Jane realized he'd come around the desk to stand beside her.

"Yes, of course. Just a little...surprised," she replied.

"And pleased, I hope."

"And pleased," she assured him with such heartfelt honesty that she surprised herself.

She hadn't been willing to admit she might be pregnant because she hadn't thought she wanted to be. But now that she knew without a doubt that there was a child growing deep inside her, she couldn't imagine anything she wanted more.

The fears and anxieties she had harbored for years hadn't disappeared completely. Not when she knew she would be raising her baby alone. Max had been so adamantly against having children. She couldn't believe her pregnancy would change his mind.

But she wasn't a frightened young girl anymore.

She was a mature woman, capable of taking care of herself and her child. A child she would never sacrifice for the security of a loveless marriage to a man who would more than likely consider its conception the unfortunate result of the *mistake* he'd made on their wedding night.

Luckily, Max was well on his way to Hong Kong, Jane thought, glancing at her watch. By now, he'd be somewhere over the Pacific Ocean. Just as she had known he would be when she'd scheduled her appointment for that afternoon.

Not only would she have two weeks in which to implement the plan she'd already begun to formulate subconsciously, there was a good chance she would also be able to hide her condition from him, perhaps indefinitely. She had never been one to condone subterfuge of any kind. But she firmly believed she would spare herself, as well as Max, a great deal of anguish by doing whatever she could to keep him from finding out about the baby.

For now, however, she knew she would do her best to pay attention to the instructions the doctor was giving her. She had always been reasonably health conscious. She tried to eat well-balanced meals and she wasn't taking any medication. She had never smoked and rarely drank alcoholic beverages. Lately, even the single glass of wine she usually enjoyed with dinner hadn't been appealing—obviously a cue her body had been sending that, thankfully, she had heeded. But she wanted to do whatever else was necessary to guarantee her baby's good health, as well as her own.

She was most concerned about the nausea she'd been suffering, often all day long. Dr. Fourneau told her it could be caused by a combination of things—

changes in hormone levels, stress and fatigue. He also assured her it probably wouldn't last much longer— perhaps another two or three weeks at the most.

In the meantime, he recommended she eat a diet high in protein and carbohydrates, drink plenty of fluids and take the prenatal vitamin supplements he would prescribe. He also advised her to get as much rest as possible, and to avoid emotionally stressful situations.

Somehow, Jane managed not to laugh out loud at the last of his suggestions. Avoiding stress, at least for the next week or two, was going to be a real challenge.

She took the prescription he'd written for the prenatal vitamins, then nodded agreeably when he told her he'd like to see her again in four weeks should she choose to have him as her obstetrician. Had she planned to stay in Seattle, she would have. But saying as much might lead to questions she didn't feel up to answering.

Wishing her well, Dr. Fourneau saw her to the door. There she was met by one of the nurses, who escorted her to the reception desk. Rather than allow a claim to be filed on her insurance, she wrote a personal check to cover the cost of the office visit. That way, no one in the human-resources department at Hamilton Enterprises, and thus Max himself via the office grapevine, would be likely to find out about her pregnancy, even inadvertently.

As she made her way from the doctor's office to the parking lot, Jane realized there was no one in Seattle she could tell about her pregnancy without word of it getting back to Max. Her few close friends were also his employees, and she didn't feel right about burdening them with such a tender secret. Not when one small slip of the tongue could do unaccountable damage to all concerned.

When Max had proposed marriage, he had made sure she understood they would not be having any children, and nothing he had said or done in the past ten weeks led her to believe he would ever change his mind. In fact, she had begun to believe he was sorry he'd weighed himself down with a *wife*.

He never sought out her company unless he had business to discuss or a social function to attend. The friendship and camaraderie she had hoped to share with him had been all but nonexistent. Sadly, living with him had turned out to be lonelier than living on her own had ever been.

She didn't think she could bear to have him suggest she have an abortion. And she certainly didn't intend to try to raise her child in such an unwelcoming environment. She had suffered Max's indifference because of the bargain she'd made. She wouldn't subject her child to it, as well.

She had learned firsthand how awful it was to live in a home where your presence was barely tolerated. No child of hers was going to grow up that way—not as long as she had the power to prevent it. Which she did, she assured herself as she climbed into her car and started the engine.

She had money in the bank to tide her over for a year or more, and she had friends—three old, dear friends—she could turn to. Any one of them would look after her child if anything happened to her. And one in particular would be more than willing to help her now.

Every time she had sent a card or letter, Emma Dalton had invited her to come back to Serenity, Texas, for a visit. Only she had stayed on in the small town where they, along with Megan and Kathleen, had spent their teenage years, making a home for herself despite the personal tragedy she'd suffered. And she had made sure they all knew they were welcome there.

Of course, Emma had meant for a week or two. But Jane was fairly certain her friend wouldn't mind if she stayed on a little longer once she explained the situation. She would call later that evening, make certain Emma's invitation was still open, then make further plans accordingly.

Leaving the parking lot, Jane guided her car into the busy flow of late-afternoon traffic wending toward downtown. She thought about going back to the office for a couple of hours, but the doctor's admonition to take it easy rang in her ears. Her meeting with the software-design group that morning had been a success, but there was no reason why she couldn't wait until tomorrow to write up her report.

She had spent the past ten weeks pushing herself to keep busy so she wouldn't have time to dwell on her unhappiness. But in a matter of moments, her life had changed immeasurably. A new and unbelievably exciting prospect lay ahead of her—one that had staked a claim on her heart and soul. She wanted to savor it with every fiber of her being.

She had never wanted to consider motherhood an option. But out of Max's mistake had come a miracle. She couldn't believe how thrilled she was. Or how terrified.

What was she getting herself into? Not only motherhood, but *single* motherhood. Yet women all over the world coped with that responsibility. She'd just have to have faith that she could, too.

She wasn't going to take anything from Max. Not even the sum agreed upon in their prenuptial contract should they divorce. She couldn't, in good conscience, and keep the baby a secret.

She had her savings, though, and no debts to speak of. Of course, after the baby came, she would have to move to Dallas or Houston and find another job. But with her background and experience, that shouldn't be too difficult.

As Jane drove along in the stop-and-go traffic, her thoughts awhirl, the enormity of what she was planning to do finally began to hit her. She was not only going to leave her husband without telling him why, she was also going to give up her high-paying job, travel halfway across the country to live with a friend she hadn't seen in years and bring a baby into the world on her own.

She, who had always guarded against the kind of foolhardy acts one often lived to regret.

But she couldn't see that she had any other choice, at least not one that wouldn't entail telling Max about the baby. And that she refused to do.

Just the thought of how horror-struck he would be was enough to make her want to weep. Why put herself through such torment when the end result would be the same? She would have to leave Seattle and make a new life for herself and her baby no matter what. She didn't want to take with her the memory of Max's anger and resentment. She'd much rather remember the kindness and concern he'd shown her last night at Parker Campion's party.

By the time Jane arrived at the front door of the apartment—having stopped first to fill her prescription at the pharmacy on the building's ground floor—she was shaking with a combination of physical and emotional fatigue. She fit her key into the lock, opened the door and stepped inside, then leaned against the foyer wall a few moments, trying to gather enough strength for the detour to the kitchen she had to make before going on to her room.

She wasn't sure what Calvin might be up to at that time of day, but common courtesy demanded that she let him know she was home. She also wanted to tell him not to bother with dinner. All she wanted was to strip off her clothes, pull on her flannel pajamas and crawl into bed.

The apartment seemed deserted, but as Jane moved toward the living room, she heard the faint sound of classical music, and a most enticing aroma teased her senses. Her stomach growled, reminding her that she'd barely nibbled at the salad and grilled fish she'd ordered at lunch. She hadn't been hungry then. Now, however, as she inhaled deeply, her mouth watered with anticipation. For the first time in weeks, she *wanted* to eat.

Just inside the kitchen doorway, Jane paused, smiling to herself as she spied Calvin standing at the stove, stirring a bubbling pot with one hand while keeping time to the music playing on the stereo with the other. Then her stomach growled again, and she couldn't help but speak her thoughts aloud.

"Whatever you're cooking, it smells wonderful."

"A light but flavorful beef broth enhanced by a medley of fresh spring vegetables and barley. At least according to the recipe I clipped from the paper the other day," he replied, smiling as he glanced over his shoulder. Eyeing her shrewdly, he added, "You're home early. Very early, as a matter of fact. Feeling a bit under the weather again?''

''More a case of the cat being away and the mouse deciding to play,'' she said, tossing her briefcase on a chair and shrugging out of her suit jacket. ''Actually, I *was* feeling a bit tired, too. But the smell of that soup has revived me. Any chance I could have a bowl right now?''

''A very good chance.'' He set the ladle on the counter and crossed to one of the cabinets to fetch a couple of bowls. ''Mind if I join you?''

''Of course not,'' she assured him, taking spoons from a drawer.

As Jane sat at the table, watching the butler arrange fresh rolls in a basket, then serve the soup, she realized she hadn't factored Calvin into her plan. Unless she could elicit his support, he would alert Max to her disappearance long before he was scheduled to return from his trip.

But could she ask him to go against his employer? She had to, she admitted. Making a clean getaway would be impossible otherwise. She needed an ally here, and at the office, as well.

She knew that Doug Jacoby, her second-in-command, along with the others on her team, could be counted on to cover for her. She hoped she could convince Calvin to do likewise.

They ate in companionable silence for several minutes. Lost in thoughts of how best to broach the subject of her impending departure, Jane reached for a second roll. Glancing up, she caught the butler watching her, a keen look in his eyes.

''You've gotten your appetite back, haven't you?'' he asked.

"At least for tonight."

"Oh, I imagine the worst of the...sickness is just about over."

Jane froze, her hand hovering over the basket of rolls, and stared at him. He knew, she thought, her heart starting to pound. How, she had no idea. But he knew that she was pregnant.

"It's all right, Jane. Your secret is safe with me. Has been for several weeks now," he assured her.

A hot flush burning her cheeks, she pulled her hand back. Wordlessly, she lowered her gaze.

"Have you seen a doctor yet?" he questioned in a gentle tone.

"Just today," she murmured.

"And...?"

"The baby's due December 23."

"Just in time for Christmas."

Risking a glance at him, she saw that he was pleased, and her spirits lightened somewhat.

"Yes, that's what the doctor said."

"When are you going to tell Max?"

"Tell...Max...?" she repeated, her heart sinking again.

Naturally, that was what Calvin would expect of her. His first loyalty belonged to Max, after all. But she couldn't allow herself to be dissuaded by that fact. She had to state her case.

"He's aware that you've been ill, but he has no idea why."

"I'm...I'm not going to tell Max about the baby," she said, tipping her chin up.

"I see. May I ask why not?"

"When he proposed marriage, he made it clear that he didn't want children, and I agreed to his terms. I didn't think I wanted children, either. Since then, my feelings have changed, but I can't expect the same to be true of Max. He was so adamant about it.'' She twisted her hands together in her lap and looked away. "I admit that alone isn't much of a reason to keep him in the dark. But I can't be sure how he'd react. What if he suggested I get rid of the baby? I couldn't bear that."

"You think Max would do that?"

"I don't honestly know. Not for sure. Do you?"

"I wouldn't like to think so, but Max has had some odd notions since Alyssa died," Calvin admitted. "And sometimes, when he feels threatened, he has a bad habit of saying things he doesn't really mean."

"I realize he's the one who pays your salary," Jane murmured, meeting his gaze again. "I don't expect you to lie—"

"As I said, your secret will be safe with me for as long as you want, and I'll help you in whatever way I can. Just let me know what you have in mind."

With a sigh of relief, Jane told Calvin about the tentative plans she'd made. She mentioned Emma, but didn't say exactly where her friend lived. She doubted Max would try to find her. Considering how distant he'd been lately, he would probably be happy to have her off his hands. But just in case he was interested enough to ask, she didn't want to add another lie to the ones Calvin would already be telling on her behalf.

They also discussed the timing of her departure. Calvin suggested she wait to leave Seattle until the last possible moment. Reluctantly, Jane agreed.

Max would be checking in periodically while he was traveling, and would expect to talk to her on those occasions. If he couldn't catch up with her at the office or the apartment, he would wonder what was going on. Calvin would only be able to cover for her a day or two without arousing his suspicions.

In addition, Jane would need time to prepare her staff for her departure. She couldn't leave them in the lurch no matter how eager she was to get away.

Calvin also advised her to put most of her personal belongings in storage. Moving them to the unit she was already renting would be easy enough. And once she was settled in a home of her own, he could arrange to have them transported.

The butler wasn't happy that she planned to drive alone to her destination, however. In fact, had he known just how far she intended to go, he probably would have withdrawn his support altogether.

But she couldn't do without a car where she was going. Not only was hers in excellent condition, but it was paid for, as well. Selling it, then buying another once she reached Serenity just didn't make sense. And driving the car herself would cost her much less than flying to Texas and having it shipped.

Granted, the long trip across the country would take several days. But she had fended for herself for so long that she was sure she could handle it on her own.

By the time Jane polished off a second bowl of soup and a slice of raspberry tart, her plans had definitely begun to take shape. Thanks to Calvin's understanding and support, she felt as if a weight had been lifted from her shoulders. All she had left to do was contact Emma.

She placed the call to her friend from her bedroom, pacing nervously as far as the telephone cord would allow as she waited for an answer. Emma seemed so pleased to hear from her that Jane suffered a momentary pang of guilt. She was expecting an awful lot of someone she hadn't seen in almost eight years. But who else could she turn to?

When Emma asked how she was enjoying married life, Jane hesitated a few seconds, then told her everything.

"Of course, you'll come and stay with me for as long as you want," Emma said, her voice matter-of-fact. "I have more than enough room for you and the baby. You'll get the best possible medical care here in Serenity, too. The hospital has doubled in size over the past few years. I can also recommend at least three doctors for you to choose from. And I'll be here for you, too."

"I can't tell you how much that means to me," Jane replied, tears filling her eyes.

Emma had always been the most sensible, as well as the most softhearted of them. Obviously, she hadn't changed a bit despite the personal tragedy she had suffered several years ago.

"Actually, I have ulterior motives," Emma teased. "The children's librarian is taking the summer off so she can join her husband on his overseas sabbatical. I'm going to need help with the weekly puppet show, story hour, arts and crafts...."

"You want me to work with children?" Jane asked, vaguely disconcerted.

She didn't mind lending a hand, but surely she would be better at shelving books, stamping cards or sending out overdue notices.

"I can't think of anyone better," Emma assured her. "Trust me, you'll love it, and the little ones will love you, too."

"I never thought I'd be much good with kids."

"Well, I have a feeling you're going to be pleasantly surprised."

Emma gave Jane what news she'd had from Megan and Kathleen over the past few weeks, then they set a tentative date for Jane's arrival, agreed to talk again in a few days to finalize the details and said goodbye.

That night, Jane slept better than she had in weeks. And in the days that followed, she kept her thoughts focused firmly on the future.

At the office, she prepared her staff for her departure as discreetly as possible, reassigning responsibility for the various projects on her desk to those most capable of seeing them to completion. She couldn't tell them she would be leaving permanently. When the time came, she would say she had personal business that would be taking her out of town indefinitely.

At the apartment, she sorted and packed her personal belongings with Calvin's help. She had room for no more than a couple of suitcases and three, maybe four, small boxes in her car. Luckily, that turned out to be all she needed for the things she most wanted to take with her.

The hardest moments were those she spent talking to Max. He called frequently, more frequently than Jane had anticipated, and his mood was always upbeat. The trip was going well, of course, but he was eager to talk about other things, too.

He seemed especially concerned about her health. Since the nausea had passed, she wasn't lying when she told him she was feeling fine. Yet she wasn't being truthful with him, not by any stretch of the imagination, and that troubled her more than she cared to admit.

As the day of her departure drew near, Jane wondered if she was doing the right thing, after all. Max seemed more and more like the man she had thought she was marrying. The warmth in his voice when he spoke to her had planted a tiny seed of hope deep in her heart, and a part of her wanted to nurture it.

But he was half a world away, she reminded herself, clinging to common sense, probably feeling lonely among so many strangers. Naturally, he would seek out the one person he could depend on to lend a sympathetic ear. And why would he be rude when a little kindness and concern had always worked to his advantage in the past?

Early in the morning two days before Max was due to return, Jane and Calvin packed the last of her things in the trunk of her car.

"You'll keep the cell phone on, right?" he prodded.

"Yes, I promise."

"And you'll call each evening to let me know you're all right?"

"No later than seven o'clock your time."

"I'll have every police officer from here to Serenity, Texas, out looking for you if you don't," he vowed.

After days of badgering, Jane had finally told the butler where she was going and the route she planned to take. She had also given him Emma's telephone number. She hadn't had the heart to worry him any more than absolutely necessary, and of course, she trusted he would keep her secret safe as promised.

"I'm going to be fine," she assured him.

"Take care of yourself and the little one."

"I will." She held out her hand to him. "Goodbye, Calvin, and thanks for...everything."

"You're more than welcome." He took her hand,

pulled her close and gave her a fatherly hug. "I'm going to miss you."

"Me, too," Jane said, swiping at the tears burning her eyes.

Reluctantly, she stepped back and turned away. She slid into the car, closed the door and started the engine. She forced herself to smile, waved to Calvin, then pulled out of her parking space and drove toward the ramp that led down to the street.

She didn't look back. Not as she rounded the first narrow curve of the ramp. Not as she turned onto the street that ran alongside the apartment building. Not as she blended into the traffic on the freeway heading south out of town.

Looking back would have been too great a temptation. She might have actually *gone* back. She'd had such hope in her heart when she'd married Max. And hope had seen her through so many tough times in the past.

But she couldn't think only of herself anymore. She had a child to consider now. A child who deserved to grow up in the most loving, caring environment she could provide. And the only way she could do that was by putting as much distance as possible between herself and Max.

Subjecting herself to his antipathy was one thing. She couldn't, *wouldn't,* do that to her baby. Never, under any circumstances at all.

Chapter Seven

Max sat alone in the back of the Lincoln TownCar, the glass partition between him and the driver raised to afford him a measure of privacy. As the car cruised slowly through the airport traffic, rain fell in a steady downpour, beating against the roof and washing over the tinted windows, making it impossible for him to see much of anything in the midafternoon gloom.

But Max wasn't really interested in the scenery. In fact, he was so deep in thought that he noticed very little of what was happening outside the car.

He was late returning to Seattle, three days late to be exact. Instead of leaving Tokyo on Wednesday and arriving home Thursday as originally planned, he had been delayed until Saturday by his Japanese host. The man had suggested they spend a few days at his country home outside the city, and Max had felt obligated to accept the hospitality he knew was rarely offered to anyone but Suzuki's most trusted business associates.

For the most part, Max had enjoyed the time they'd spent together. But as one day followed another, and he couldn't seem to catch up with Jane either at the office or the apartment, a niggle of anxiety had taken root in his subconscious. She was out, always *out*, but no one knew where, not even Calvin.

When Max had called the office Wednesday to say he would be delayed, hearing that she wasn't there hadn't really concerned him in the least. He had left a message with her secretary, then called the apartment to advise Calvin, as well. He hadn't had an opportunity to check back again until he returned to Tokyo Saturday morning.

Max had called the apartment then, but Calvin had told him Jane wasn't there. He had asked where she was, but the butler had said he didn't know. Max had thought that was odd. Where would Jane have gone on a Friday night without telling Calvin?

Unfortunately, he hadn't time to question the butler further. He had advised him of his new arrival time, then rung off so he could finish packing.

Max's flight had landed in Seattle on time, but clearing customs had taken what seemed like an eternity. He had been more eager than usual to collect his luggage and be on his way. But then, he hadn't expected to be met by a driver from the limousine service he used for trips to and from the airport.

Since it was a Sunday, Max had thought Jane would be there waiting for him, not a uniformed chauffeur holding a sign with Hamilton Enterprises printed on it. Granted, the nasty weather could have kept her from coming. But that didn't lessen his disappointment.

He knew it was foolish of him. He hadn't actually asked her to be there. He had just hoped that she would come because she wanted to.

Now, staring at the cars zooming past the slower moving limo, Max realized he had been expecting quite a lot of Jane. She couldn't read his mind, so how would she know he'd had a change of heart?

Being with her again, not only as a friend but as a lover, had been all he'd been able to think about during the time they'd been apart. Yet he'd never once said as much to her. He had wanted to do that face-to-face. But he had tried to relay his feelings in other ways, apparently with less success than he'd thought.

At the apartment building, the driver pulled under the porte cochere, opened the car door for Max, then fetched his luggage from the trunk. The doorman took over from there, asking politely about his trip abroad as they rode up in the elevator. At the penthouse door, Max thanked the man for his help, then fit his key into the lock and let himself in. As he carried his suitcases across the threshold, Calvin appeared in the foyer.

''Plane a little late getting in?'' the butler asked, relieving him of one of his bags.

''Actually, the plane was on time, but going through customs was a real pain.''

Max looked past Calvin as the butler led the way into the living room. A couple of lamps were lit to ward off the dreariness of the day, but the room itself was deserted.

''Where's Jane?'' he asked, frowning as he halted in midstride.

''She's gone, Max.''

Something about the butler's tone and the steely look in his eyes as he paused, too, sent warning bells ringing somewhere in the back of Max's mind. Slowly, he set down the suitcase he'd been carrying.

"What do you mean by *gone?*" he asked, his voice sounding oddly unsteady to his ears.

"Just what I said."

"Gone *where?*" Max demanded. "And for how long?"

"I can't really say."

"What the hell is *that* supposed to mean?" Frustrated, Max propped his hands on his hips and glared at the butler. "You don't know where she went and how long she'll be gone, or you know, but for some reason I can't fathom, you're unable to tell me?"

"She left a letter for you on your dresser," Calvin said, continuing on toward the hallway. "I'm sure it will answer at least some of your questions."

Max grabbed his suitcase and followed after him, his thoughts whirling. Jane hadn't indicated that she was seriously disturbed about anything before he'd left for Hong Kong. She had been quieter than usual, both at home and at the office, but she hadn't seemed to be *pouting.* He remembered thinking that she had seemed rather weary, but he'd chalked that up to her busy schedule.

As far as Max could see, *he* hadn't given her any reason to run off without an explanation. He had been holding up his end of their bargain, hadn't he? So what had caused her to renege? And why hadn't she talked to him about it first?

He had never intended for her to be unhappy. He would have been willing to go along with almost anything she wanted. All she would have had to do was tell him.

For her to just pick up and go was so totally out of

character. Unless something outside his control had occurred to upset her.

"What I'd like are some answers from *you*, Calvin," Max pressed. "What the hell happened here while I was away?"

"Nothing that I'm aware of, sir."

"Well, *something* must have—"

Just outside the doorway to Jane's suite, Max froze, his eyes widening in dismay. What he could see of the sitting room was empty, totally, completely empty. Not a stick of furniture remained.

"Oh, no..." he muttered, a sinking feeling in the pit of his stomach.

Jane hadn't gone away temporarily to work out some personal problem. Evidently, she had gone for good.

"Read the letter she left, Max. Then we'll talk," Calvin advised.

He set the suitcase he'd been carrying just inside Max's bedroom doorway, then retraced his path down the hallway, giving his employer a wide berth.

Max wondered what the butler thought he would do. More than likely, his desire to grab him and shake the truth out of him showed on his face. Max didn't care. He wasn't in the mood to hide his emotions. And at that moment, anger was quickly taking the place of the hurt that had stabbed at his heart only a few moments ago.

So Jane had decided to take off. So what? He had gotten along just fine on his own for eight years. He could see no reason why he couldn't do so again. They had been together...what? Only six and a half months counting their engagement. Not all that long in the general scheme of things. Certainly not long enough for her absence to make any real impact on him.

Thank heavens he'd had the forethought to insist they sign a prenuptial agreement. That would make the process of divorcing her relatively simple. She would be entitled to the agreed-upon settlement, of course. Not a huge amount of money, but enough to guarantee her comfort in the future.

Now that he thought about it, that was probably what she had been after all along. A nice little nest egg to make her life easy. She hadn't stuck around to talk out her problems because she hadn't had any. She had simply bided her time until she could leave him without any hassle.

He should have realized she wasn't nearly as sweet or as innocent as she'd pretended to be. Savvy businessman that he'd always prided himself on being, he should have known she had an agenda all her own. But no, he had fallen for her act hook, line and sinker.

Max spied the heavy vellum envelope propped on his dresser as he walked into the bedroom. He had half a mind to toss it in the trash unopened. What could she possibly have to say that would be of any interest to him?

He dropped his suitcase next to the one Calvin had left and strode across the room. He grabbed the envelope, weighed it in his hand for several seconds, then lifted the flap and removed the two sheets of matching stationery neatly folded and tucked within.

Two sheets. More than he thought she would need to say whatever she had to say, he mused as he eyed her familiar script.

Max:

I realize I'm taking the coward's way out, but I thought it would be easier for both of us. A face-to-face confrontation would have been so distressful, and I believe the result would have been the same.

I wanted our marriage to work, and I assume you did, too. But in all honesty, it hasn't.

I know we made a bargain and I've tried to live up to my part of it, but I can't go on as I have been any longer. You haven't been happy and neither have I, so I thought it would be best if I left Seattle.

I have taken the liberty of putting Doug Jacoby in charge of the marketing department until your return. He is more than qualified for the job. He will be able to update you on the status of the various projects already under way.

I have also hired a lawyer to act on my behalf in the divorce proceedings. Please send any paperwork to him. He will see that I receive it. I also want you to know that I don't feel right about accepting any money from you. We were together such a brief time. You don't really owe me anything in that respect.

I'm sorry things didn't work out the way you had hoped. Perhaps you'll find the happiness you deserve with someone else. Take care...

Jane

Below her signature on the second page was the name, address and telephone number of a Seattle attorney Max wasn't familiar with.

A frown creasing his forehead, he walked over to the bed and sat down wearily, still gripping her letter in his hand. He was ashamed of himself for even thinking she had used their marriage as a means to personal profit. He had known her better than that. She was a kind, generous, honest young woman. If anyone had done any using, it was him. And apparently she'd had all she could take.

She could have said something, though. Anything to let him know she wanted their relationship to change.

Somewhere in the back of his mind, he knew he wasn't being fair to her. In fact, he had no right at all to blame her. *He* was the one who had made a mess of things from the very start. Saying one thing, then doing another.

But she could have *told* him how she was feeling weeks ago. Then he would have had a chance to make it up to her. Instead, she had run off the moment his back was turned.

Well, fine. She wanted her freedom, she could damned well have it. So their marriage hadn't worked out. Big deal. He'd get over it after a while. It wasn't as if he'd ever been in love with her.

Angry all over again, Max tossed the letter aside, stood and headed toward the bathroom. Jane had left of her own volition, as she'd had every right to do, and there wasn't much he could do about it.

He certainly wasn't chasing after her. That was for sure. He didn't have time for that kind of game. He had a business to run, and after two weeks away, he was going to have a lot of catching up to do. Especially with his vice president of marketing God only knew where.

Max showered, dressed in faded jeans and an old sweatshirt, then went to the kitchen to get something to eat. He found the table set for one, a bottle of his favorite red wine already open. Three chafing dishes, candles flickering, had been left on the counter for him, too. Apparently, Calvin had decided to stay out of his way.

He would have to assure the butler that he bore him no hard feelings. It hadn't been fair to expect the man to choose between him and Jane. Not when he'd encouraged Calvin to befriend her from the very beginning.

He poured a glass of wine, then lifted the covers on the dishes. One of his favorite meals—beef Stroganoff with egg noodles and steamed asparagus. His mouth watered in anticipation.

Wondering if Calvin had eaten, Max crossed to the doorway of his quarters and looked in. Calvin sat in his recliner, a book open on his lap. He glanced up, then stood hurriedly.

"Everything all right, sir?" he asked in his most reserved tone of voice.

"Just fine, Calvin. But there's more than enough for two. Why don't you join me? Unless you've already had dinner..."

"I appreciate the invitation, but I'm not very hungry this evening."

Max frowned as he eyed the butler narrowly. Calvin looked back steadily. Max blinked first, shifting uncomfortably under the older man's scrutiny.

"I'm sorry I took my anger out on you when I first got home. Finding out that Jane had gone really threw me for a few moments there."

"Only a few moments, sir?"

Max shoved a hand in the back pocket of his jeans and gulped a mouthful of wine.

"Obviously, she wasn't happy here, but she didn't want to stay and work things out. I'm not thrilled that she left me, but I'm not going to let it get me down, either."

"Oh, I'd never expect you to do *that*," Calvin muttered.

Needled by the sarcasm in his butler's voice, Max glared at him.

"If you have something to say to me, why don't you just say it?"

"Because I'd rather not waste my time."

"Fine, suit yourself. Just don't expect me to wander around like some poor lost soul because my wife of three months walked out on me."

Max turned and strode back to the kitchen, poured another glass of wine and served himself from the chafing dishes. The food was delicious, but he hardly tasted the little he actually ate.

After a while, he pushed his plate away, but he continued to sit at the table, refilling his wineglass again. By the time Calvin came to clear away the dishes, Max should have been feeling no pain. Instead, he had the oddest urge to put his head down and cry.

"Where did she go, Calvin?" he asked, pushing his empty glass aside and standing.

"Why do you want to know? So you can go after her?"

"Hell, no, I'm not going after her. I just want to know where she went. Call me curious."

"There are a lot of things I'd like to call you, Max. Right now, curious isn't one of them," the butler replied.

"Damn it, where did she go?" Max growled.

"I don't see any reason why you need to know. Not in your present frame of mind."

"She's my wife. I have a right to know."

"Your *beloved* wife, Max? The woman you intend to *honor* and *cherish* all the days of your life?"

Wordlessly, Max turned his back on the butler. Hands clenched at his sides, he headed toward the kitchen doorway.

"Unless that's how you think of her, leave her in peace. Please, Max, for her sake."

He tried to block out Calvin's words, but they spun in his head over and over as he stalked across the living room.

Your beloved wife...the woman you intend to honor and cherish...honor and cherish all the days of your life....

That wasn't what he had wanted six months ago, and it wasn't what he wanted now. He had been in love once, and when that love had been lost to him forever, he'd raged and wept like a helpless child. He had never wanted to be possessed by such torturous emotions again. And he wasn't going to be.

Jane Elliott Hamilton could go to the devil for all he cared.

In the hallway, he paused just long enough to shut the door to her empty suite of rooms. Then, his head pounding, he continued on to his bedroom. Thick gray clouds blotted out whatever daylight was left, and rain beat relentlessly against the windows.

Unable to see much in the semidarkness, he stumbled over the suitcases still standing just inside the doorway. Muttering angrily, he kicked out at them, cursed when his bare foot connected with solid leather, then limped to the bed.

He sat on the edge of the mattress and stared at Jane's letter, lying where he'd left it, the creamy sheets of stationery the only bright spot in the room. After several moments, he reached out, grasped the pages in his hand and crushed them as he made a fist.

He had meant to toss the letter on the floor, but he couldn't seem to make himself let go. Still clutching it, he stretched out on the bed, fully clothed, and stared at the ceiling, his thoughts growing more muddled and more maudlin.

Too much wine, he told himself, slinging an arm over his eyes. A toxic combination when added to jet lag. He'd been up almost twenty-four hours. Was it any wonder his defenses were down?

What he needed now was a good night's sleep. Then, come morning, he would be able to deal with Jane's departure in a mature and sensible manner.

Somewhere in the apartment, a telephone began to ring. Max heard it as if from a great distance. He thought about picking up the extension on the nightstand, but he didn't have the energy.

There wasn't anyone he wanted to talk to, anyway. Well, almost anyone, he amended. But why would *she* be calling here? She had already said what she'd had to say, hadn't she?

Rolling onto his stomach, Max buried his face in a pillow, Jane's letter still in his hand. With a low groan, he closed his eyes, giving in to the exhaustion that dragged at his mind and body.

Finally, fitfully, he slept.

Chapter Eight

"Good evening. Hamilton residence."

"Hi, it's me," Jane said. Hearing Calvin's voice come across the telephone line, she settled onto one of the stools near the counter in Emma Dalton's kitchen and breathed a sigh of relief. She'd been afraid Max would answer, but she couldn't worry Calvin by failing to keep her promise. "I arrived at Emma's, safe and sound, about an hour ago."

"I'm so glad to hear that. No problems along the way?" he asked, his concern for her as obvious as it had been every night they had spoken since she'd left Seattle.

"None at all."

She had driven through a patch of thunderstorms along the Texas–New Mexico border that had forced her to stop earlier than she'd planned yesterday afternoon. But the weather had been clear for the remainder of her drive.

"And your friend Emma? Was she happy to see you?"

"Oh, yes," Jane assured him, smiling as she recalled Emma's tearful embrace.

Throughout her journey, Jane had wondered just how warm her welcome would be. By that afternoon, she had been prepared to stay only a day or two. But Emma had been waiting on the front-porch swing, looking much the same as she had the last time Jane had seen her, her mass of chin-length, curly red hair framing her delicate features in artful disarray, her bright green eyes sparkling with mischief behind the lenses of her gold wire-rimmed glasses.

Jane had had barely enough time to slide out of the car before her friend had joined her at the curb. And any doubts she'd had faded instantly when Emma put her arms around her and hugged her tearfully.

The years had fallen away, and suddenly Jane was swept back to the days when she and Emma had shared a special closeness. Neither time nor distance had broken the bond they'd forged when they'd lived together in the same foster home during their teen years.

"I'm so happy you're here...so very, very happy," Emma had said, and Jane had known she'd meant it from the bottom of her heart.

"So you'll be staying with her until the baby comes?" Calvin prodded.

"At the very least," Jane assured him. She hesitated a moment, twirling the telephone cord around her fingers, then gave in to her own curiosity. "I was wondering...has Max gotten home yet?"

Calvin had mentioned her husband's last-minute change of plans. That he had been away a few days longer than anticipated had been to her benefit. But she had been concerned about him, traveling so far from home. And now she also wondered how he had reacted to her absence.

"A couple of hours ago," Calvin said.

"Where is he now?" she asked, hoping that he wasn't within listening distance.

"Judging by the empty wine bottle I just tossed in the recycling bin, passed out in the bedroom, snoring away."

"Oh, dear," Jane murmured. Max rarely drank more than a glass or two of wine with his meal. "Was he…upset about my…departure?"

"He looked like he'd been gut-punched when he saw that your suite was empty. I'm assuming he read the letter you left for him. He didn't say anything about it, but he spent a good deal of time stomping around like a mad bull with a poker up his… Well, you get the picture."

"Mmm, yes."

"Didn't eat much dinner, but as I said, he drank quite a bit of wine. Finally got around to asking if I knew where you went. I didn't tell him, but I think maybe it would be a good idea—"

"No, please don't," she begged. "He hasn't had time to get used to the idea that I'm gone yet. Once he does, I'm sure he'll realize it's for the best. I don't want him to feel obligated to me in any way. Then he might just decide to check up on me. Especially if he knows where I am. And if he does that, we both know he's not going to like what he finds."

"I'm not so sure—"

"Well, I am," Jane cut in again, her voice edging up a notch. "Please, Calvin, you promised."

"Yes, I know," he assured her quietly. "And I always keep my word."

"Thank you," she replied. Then, sensing his hesitancy, and fearing that if he pressed her further, she'd give in, she added, "I'd better go now. Emma's probably wondering what's happened to me."

"You'll keep in touch, won't you?"

"I'm not sure that's such a good idea."

"Just drop me a note every now and then so I'll know you're all right, and I'll do the same."

Reluctantly, Jane agreed. Breaking all ties would probably be better, but she didn't want to hurt Calvin's feelings. He had been so good to her, and she knew his concern for her was heartfelt.

After saying goodbye to him, Jane cradled the receiver, then went in search of Emma. Her friend had retreated to the front-porch swing. Jane joined her there, settling onto the cushioned seat with a weary sigh.

"Something wrong?" Emma asked, seeming to sense her anxiety.

"Not exactly," Jane hedged as she twisted the wedding band she still wore on her ring finger around and around.

"Want to talk about it?" Gently, Emma put a hand over Jane's, stilling her fretful fidgeting.

"I didn't think leaving Max would be so...unsettling. I didn't feel I had much choice under the circumstances. I wanted my baby to grow up in a loving home, and considering Max's stand on having children, I didn't think that would be possible if I stayed with him."

Pausing, Jane stared into the growing darkness for several moments. Beyond Emma's house, the narrow, tree-lined street was Sunday-night quiet. Through the windows of her neighbors' homes, lights cast a warm glow on the neatly manicured lawns. The scent of the flowers in Emma's old-fashioned English garden drifted across the porch on a cool breeze.

It was so peaceful there, so...serene. But she couldn't seem to calm down. Her conversation with Calvin, centering as it had on Max, had left her mind in turmoil.

"I didn't intend to cause Max any grief, though," she continued. "In fact, I didn't think I *could*. He was so distant the past three months. So...cool and...aloof. He didn't really seem to care about me one way or another. I thought he'd be relieved that I left without making demands or causing a scene."

"But he isn't?"

"Not from what Calvin said. He drank too much at dinner tonight, and he's only done that one other time that I can recall."

"When was that?"

"On our wedding night," Jane admitted rather sheepishly.

"Sounds to me like he isn't completely immune to your charms," Emma teased in a kindly tone.

"He wanted to know where I went, but Calvin wouldn't tell him," Jane added, ignoring Emma's remark.

"Maybe you should contact him and see what he says. Unless *you* don't want anything more to do with him."

"Oh, no. I miss him. Much more than I thought I would. And at the oddest moments, I find myself imagining what it would be like to tell him about the baby and see his eyes light up with joy. But I know that wouldn't be the way he'd react. Don't get me wrong, Emma. He's not an ogre. He doesn't dislike children as a matter of principle. He just doesn't want any of his own.''

''Did he ever tell you why?''

''Not really, but I gather it has something to do with his first wife's death. She was pregnant, and the baby died, too. I don't know the details, but I do know he loved her very much.''

''Unlike you, huh?''

''Yes, unlike me. But he made that clear when he proposed. He wanted a marriage of convenience only, and that's what I agreed to.''

''Yet he made love to you on your wedding night. Very interesting,'' Emma murmured. Then she added in a more matter-of-fact tone, ''You know, when you first told me the truth about your marriage to Max, I have to admit I was appalled. I couldn't believe you would settle for that kind of arrangement. You're young, you're lovely and you're so smart.''

''I was lonely...so lonely, Emma, and I didn't think I was capable of being a real wife to any man. Just the thought of having sex made me cringe,'' Jane admitted.

''But not with Max. Obviously...'' Gesturing toward Jane's tummy, Emma laughed.

''I'm not sure exactly what happened during the three months of our engagement, but on our wedding night, when he took me to bed—'' Jane shrugged and shook her head ''—I wanted to be with him in every way. We had grown so close, and he had always been kind and considerate. I knew that he would never hurt me. And he didn't. He made me feel whole again.

"But then, the next morning, he acted as if he had made a big mistake, and he never touched me again."

"Maybe making love to you meant more to him than he's willing to admit, and that scares him," Emma suggested.

"Oh, how I wish..." Jane smiled and shook her head again. "Still a hopeless romantic, aren't you?"

"At least where my friends are concerned."

Recalling Emma's loss almost three years ago, Jane shifted on the swing and slipped an arm around her shoulders.

"I know you'll never forget Teddy, but you'll fall in love again some day, probably when you least expect it."

Looking away for a long moment, Emma said nothing. Then she met Jane's gaze again, a bright smile tilting the corners of her mouth, and neatly changed the subject.

"Why don't we get you settled in your room? I know you must be tired, and we've got a full day ahead of us tomorrow. I've taken the day off so I can show you around town. You won't believe how Serenity has grown. Since you'll have to choose a doctor soon, I've also taken the liberty of making appointments with the three I mentioned. You can take a looksee, then decide which one you like best. Also, Margaret insisted we join her for lunch."

"Wow, you *have* been busy." Jane smiled, too. "Thanks, friend."

"My pleasure."

"Seeing Teddy's mother again will be especially nice. I'm so glad the two of you are still close."

"Margaret has been really good to me," Emma stated simply.

"And Teddy's brother? How is he?"

"I don't really know. Sam hasn't come back to Serenity since...since Teddy died, and Margaret hasn't said much about him lately." Averting her gaze, Emma stood briskly and pulled Jane to her feet. "Come on, let's go inside. I baked a peach pie this morning. Think the little one would enjoy a slice?"

Aware that she had ventured into territory her friend would rather not explore, Jane followed Emma's lead, allowing herself to be diverted.

"I don't know about the little one," she replied as she patted her tummy, "but I certainly would."

As Emma brewed a pot of herbal tea, then served up generous portions of fresh peach pie topped with scoops of vanilla ice cream, Jane finally began to relax.

Coming to Serenity had been the right thing to do. She was sorry Max was upset. But once he got over his initial surprise, she doubted her absence would affect him. In fact, six months from now—about the time the baby was due—there was a good chance he'd hardly be thinking about her at all anymore.

And that would be best...not only for her and Max, but also for their child.

Chapter Nine

Max managed to pretend that Jane's absence didn't affect him for almost a month.

He started off well enough, going to the office early that Monday morning following his arrival home and conducting the weekly staff meeting as if nothing had changed, either in his personal life or at Hamilton Enterprises. He tried not to notice the odd looks directed his way by the staff of the marketing department in general, and Doug Jacoby in particular, especially when he took the young man aside and asked him to carry on as he had since Jane's departure. From then on, however, it was an uphill battle.

Max knew he should offer Jacoby Jane's title along with the raise in salary he'd stipulated, but he couldn't bring himself to replace her in such a permanent way. As one week became two, he kept telling himself she would get whatever had been bugging her out of her system and come back to him, ready—perhaps even eager—to resume her role as his wife again. More than that, he *fantasized* about it.

One minute, Max would imagine Jane walking into his office, looking cool and elegant in one of her classy little suits; the next, he would envision her curled up on a sofa at the apartment, a welcoming smile teasing at the corners of her mouth. But whimsy failed to become reality as another week passed.

Despite the piles of paperwork cluttering his desk—the contracts ready to be reviewed, the research-and-development strategies waiting to be honed—by the end of July, Max was spending most days at the office staring out the window for hours at a time. And when he returned to the apartment, he paced like a caged animal, the silence weighing on him like a sharp-edged stone.

Never one to keep his disapproval to himself, Calvin spoke to him only when absolutely necessary, and then in the deferential tone that had always ground on Max's nerves. In the past, Max had always been able to redeem himself within a day or two. Now, however, he knew better than to expect absolution. His transgression had not been a minor one. Not only had he driven his wife away, but he had also added insult to injury by pretending not to care.

Indeed, *pretending* summed up exactly what he had done for most of the month of July. Outside, summer breezes warmed the air, but the desolation that had settled in his soul only seemed to deepen.

Finally, Max admitted he would have no peace until he knew where Jane had gone. He would find that out, and no more, he told himself as he made the short drive to the office on the last Monday in July.

He wouldn't go groveling to Calvin, though. He had to maintain some sense of pride, and Calvin would only start in again with all that nonsense about love. Love had nothing to do with why he wanted to find Jane. Nothing at all.

Following the staff meeting, Max called Doug Jacoby into his office.

"Have you heard from Mrs. Hamilton since she left?" he began casually enough once his secretary had shut the door.

"No, sir, I haven't." Jacoby shifted nervously from one foot to the other, but he didn't look away.

"Did she say anything about where she was going or how long she would be away?"

"No, sir. Nothing at all." The young man shrugged and shook his head, then added, "I just assumed she wasn't planning on coming back at all."

"Well, if she should contact you for any reason, please let me know," Max instructed.

"Of course, sir."

Max nodded, then gestured toward the door, indicating the interview was over.

Jacoby eyed him quizzically for several seconds. Max could almost read his mind.

You are the president and chief executive officer of Hamilton Enterprises, a multinational corporation, and you don't have any idea where your wife has gone?

Max's face flamed with embarrassment. He must look like a complete idiot to the young man. Instinctively, he wanted to defend himself, but he knew he would only end up making matters worse. There wasn't much he could honestly say for himself. He had driven his wife away, and that was that.

After Doug Jacoby finally sidled out of his office,

Max took Jane's letter from his briefcase. He smoothed the crumpled stationery, trying to make out the name of the lawyer she had hired to represent her.

Geoffrey Dubbs, Esquire. His office was located just a few blocks away, Max noted. Jane had also written down his telephone number.

Max picked up the receiver and placed the call himself. Injecting a note of urgency into his voice, he convinced the receptionist to make an appointment for him to meet with the man at two that afternoon. With luck, he might be able to get some information out of him. Any clue to Jane's whereabouts would be better than what he had now.

Too restless to bother with lunch, Max whiled away the time before his appointment with Dubbs going over Jane's personnel file.

Until recently, he hadn't realized how little he knew about her beyond her educational and business background. He remembered she had mentioned once that her parents were dead and she had no other relatives, but that was all the personal information she'd offered him.

On her employee information sheet Max saw that she had left the *Notify In Case Of An Emergency* line blank. How strange, and sad, that she hadn't been able to name someone she thought would care enough to come to her aid.

Jane had never really talked about any friends other than the people she knew at the office, and Max had never gotten the impression she was especially close to any of them. If she hadn't told Doug Jacoby where she was going, he seriously doubted she would have confided in anyone else at Hamilton Enterprises.

Max made a note to ask Calvin for the list of people

to whom wedding invitations had been sent. He recalled that Jane had added the names of several friends living out of town, none of whom had attended. Perhaps one of them might know where she'd gone.

Looking through her file more closely, Max followed the path she had taken from high school in the town of Serenity, Texas, where she was valedictorian of her class, to the University of Texas in Austin, then Stanford University in California, both via scholarships. She had worked at a variety of part-time jobs to help make ends meet, as well. And after Stanford, she'd come to work for him.

Max didn't know if Jane still had ties to anyone in Texas or California. She had never offered that kind of information about herself, and pompous, self-centered son of a bitch that he'd been, he had never bothered to ask.

Looking back at the way he'd behaved toward her, Max had to admit it was a wonder she'd put up with him for as long as she had. What had prompted her allegiance? Her determination to honor her part of the agreement they'd made?

But if that were true, surely she would still be there, trying to work through whatever problem she'd had. Fleeing the way she had—without the slightest word of warning—seemed totally out of character. What had caused her to do so?

Max was almost afraid to find out.

His meeting with Geoffrey Dubbs only added to his frustration. The short, stout man, dressed in a rumpled suit, his thinning hair standing on end as if regularly raked by careless fingers, greeted him with an absent-minded smile and a congenial handshake. But his air of affability disappeared the moment he sat behind his paper-strewed desk and fixed Max with a steely gaze.

"How can I help you, Mr. Hamilton?" he asked politely.

"I understand my wife, Jane, has hired you to represent her," Max said, his tone challenging as he looked back at the lawyer.

"That is correct, sir. As Mrs. Hamilton has requested, I will be acting as her liaison during your divorce proceedings. Once you've filed the necessary papers, of course."

"There aren't going to be any divorce proceedings," Max snapped, unaccountably annoyed by the man's ingratiating manner. Dubbs arched an eyebrow, but otherwise did not respond to Max's statement.

Goaded, Max added, "I have no intention of divorcing my wife. We had a simple misunderstanding, one I can easily rectify."

"And you would like me to relay that information to her?"

"What I would *like*..." Max began, then caught himself just in time.

He needed Dubbs's help. He wouldn't get it by making rude remarks. The lawyer was only doing his job, protecting his client as best he could. But Jane didn't need to be protected from him. He loved—

Startled by the trail his thoughts had taken, Max frowned and looked away.

"Yes, Mr. Hamilton?" Dubbs prompted. "You'd like...what?"

Drawn back to their conversation, Max pulled himself together. He cared for Jane. He cared for her a great deal. And he was concerned about her well-being. But that was all. Any deeper, more binding emotion was beyond him now. And that was exactly the way he wanted it.

"I would like to tell her myself, preferably face-to-face," he replied.

"I'll be more than happy to let her know you'd prefer to meet with her in person," Dubbs said. "If she's agreeable, we can set up a mutually acceptable time and place."

"Why don't you save us both the aggravation, and tell me where she is right now? I can take it from there."

"I'm not able to do that, Mr. Hamilton. Mrs. Hamilton is my client, and one of the things she asked of me was that I keep her whereabouts strictly confidential."

"But why?" Max demanded, making no effort to hide his puzzlement as he pushed out of his chair.

He paced away from the lawyer's desk, then turned and faced the man again, waiting impatiently for him to answer.

"She didn't give me a reason," Dubbs said, sitting back and eyeing him warily.

Max had a fairly good idea of what he had left unspoken. Jane hadn't given him a reason, but considering how irrationally her husband was behaving, Dubbs didn't need one.

Mentally cursing his loss of control, Max drew a deep breath, then another. No matter how he tried to browbeat the man, Geoffrey Dubbs wasn't going to give him the information he wanted.

"Look, Dubbs, I'm sorry I came on so strong, but I'm worried about my wife."

"I can see that, Mr. Hamilton. But surely you understand there is only so much I can do to help you without betraying Mrs. Hamilton's trust.''

''Yes, of course I do,'' Max admitted.

He also appreciated the lawyer's tenacity where Jane's best interests were concerned. Obviously, she had put herself in good hands. But that didn't lessen Max's resentment much at all.

''As I said, I'll be happy to relay a message for you.'' Dubbs dug through the pile of papers on his desk, retrieved a legal pad, a pen and an envelope and held them out. ''You're welcome to use one of the empty offices if you'd like to write a personal note.''

Max had never been that good at putting words on paper. What if she misinterpreted his meaning in some way? He wouldn't be there to offer answers to any worrisome questions she might have. More than likely, he'd end up blowing whatever chance he had of winning her back by writing down the wrong thing.

There was also a possibility that she might go even deeper into hiding if she knew he was looking for her. Max certainly didn't want her doing that. Not now that he'd finally realized what his original course of action should have been all along.

''Actually, I don't think that will be necessary,'' Max hedged. ''Why don't you just let her know I'm concerned about her?''

''And the divorce? Will you be going forward with it, after all?''

''Tell her I'd like to give it more thought before I take any definite action.'' Thinking quickly, Max sat in the chair again, withdrew his checkbook from his coat pocket and wrote out a check in Jane's name. ''You can forward this to her, as well. Tell her to use it for any expenses she might incur while I'm making up my mind.''

Should she cash it, Max would have a way to trace her.

Dubbs glanced at the check, his eyes widening at the substantial sum, then set it aside carefully. Max could only hope it wouldn't get lost in the shuffle.

''I'll see that she gets your message and the check just as soon as possible,'' the lawyer said.

''Thank you.'' Max stood again, as did Dubbs, and offered the man his hand. ''I'll be in touch as soon as I've made a decision about the divorce.''

''I'll look forward to hearing from you then.''

Max walked the few blocks back to his office as swiftly as he could, barely mindful of the light drizzle that had begun to fall. He had wasted most of the day asking questions of people who either didn't have or wouldn't divulge the answers he needed when he should have gone straight to someone who acquired information for a living.

His only other alternative was Calvin Kerner, but he still considered the butler his last resort. Paying someone to find Jane would be much easier on his ego than going to Calvin and humbling himself as he knew he would have to.

Max wasted no time calling Randall Clove into his office. The former FBI agent was now in charge of Hamilton Enterprises's security. As Max had hoped, he was able to suggest a reputable private investigator—another former federal agent by the name of Frank Denny—who would likely be able to help him find his wife.

Denny agreed to see Max late that afternoon. He seemed competent enough, and while he made no promises, the investigator assured Max he would do everything possible to locate Jane as quickly and quietly as possible.

Max met with him again the next morning, bringing with him the pitifully small amount of information about her he'd managed to gather. Since her credit cards and bank account had been in her name only, he hadn't any access to them. In addition, she hadn't withdrawn any funds from the joint account he'd set up after their marriage, and Calvin had tossed the list of people to whom wedding invitations had been sent.

Time dragged by after that. Denny hadn't given any indication how long he thought his search would take, but Max had expected to hear something within a day or two. Every time his telephone rang, his heart leaped in anticipation. Every time he hung up—having talked to someone other than Denny—his frustration grew.

How could one woman be so damned hard to find?

After a week, Max began to ask Frank Denny just that—often on a daily basis. The investigator had no answer for him. At least none that Max found satisfactory.

When almost three weeks had passed since his first meeting with Denny, and he still had no word of Jane, Max decided the time had finally come to talk to Calvin. Working back from Seattle, Washington, to Palo Alto, California, to Austin, Texas, the investigator had come up with zip. And Jane had yet to cash the check he'd written, thus offering no clue to her whereabouts in that way.

Prowling around his office, pausing intermittently to stare at the clouds gathering over the bay late on a Wednesday afternoon, Max ignored the ringing of his telephone. He had told his secretary to screen his calls and not to bother him except in an emergency. Preparing to beg and plead with his butler was no easy task.

The phone stopped ringing, but after a moment, his intercom buzzed.

"Frank Denny calling for you, Mr. Hamilton," Ada Johns announced. "He says it's important."

"Probably wants another advance against expenses," Max muttered as he returned to his desk.

He thanked Ada, then picked up the receiver.

"This better be worth my time, Denny."

"Oh, it is. Believe me," the investigator replied.

"Yeah, sure," Max growled, trying hard not to get his hopes up. "I've heard that before."

"Well, I'm assuming you're still interested in locating your wife."

Max stood beside his desk, holding the receiver in a death grip as tension thrummed through him.

"I am."

"Well, then, you might want to jot down this address."

Almost afraid to breathe, Max pulled a pad of paper and a pen across his desk.

"Where is she?"

"Staying with a friend in some little town in Texas. Security…no, Serenity. Serenity, Texas. The woman's name is Emma Dalton, and her address is 1209 Bay Leaf Lane. I've got a telephone number, too."

His heart pounding and his hand shaking, Max wrote down all the information, repeating everything twice to make sure he'd gotten it right.

"She's all right?" he asked, finally setting his pen aside.

"Who? Emma Dalton? Far as my man could determine. She works at the library."

"My wife," Max growled. "Is my wife all right?"

"Oh, yeah, she's fine. Working at the library several days a week, too, but otherwise, keeping a pretty low profile. Took my man a while to track her down. Lots of new people in town who weren't around when she lived there twelve years ago. Apparently, she stayed in some sort of foster home back then, but the couple who ran it moved away in the late eighties."

"I see," Max murmured, his relief at having finally found his wife almost palpable.

"Anything else I can do for you, Mr. Hamilton?"

"No, I'll take it from here."

"I'm assuming you're going after her."

"Yes, I am."

"Would you like me to have my man keep an eye on her until you get there?"

"Yes, you'd better do that," Max agreed.

While it sounded as if Jane had made a new life for herself in Serenity, Texas, he didn't want to run the risk of having her disappear again in the time it would take him to get there.

"As soon as you make contact with her, I'll have him head back to Seattle," Denny advised.

"That will be fine. Thank you."

Max hung up, then buzzed Ada and told her to make whatever arrangements were necessary to get him from Seattle to Serenity, Texas, the following day. By the time he left the office, he had a first-class airline ticket to San Antonio, a rent-a-car voucher and a map of the state marked with the route from San Antonio to Serenity.

At the apartment that evening, he thought about telling Calvin his plans, but then decided against it. Though he couldn't be absolutely sure, he had a sneaking suspicion that Calvin had been in touch with Jane over the past few weeks. Should he be right, there was a possibility the butler might take it upon himself to warn her that her husband was headed her way.

Since he could easily slip away without alerting Calvin that he was going anywhere but to his office, that's what Max chose to do. Any calls to him there would be routed through Ada, who had been instructed to say only that he was away from his desk.

Much as he hated creeping off like a criminal, Max didn't want anything to get in the way of his finally seeing Jane face-to-face. The past seven weeks had been among the longest and loneliest in his life.

He hadn't been so bereft since Alyssa's death, he admitted as he packed a small carry-on bag with a change of clothes and toiletries.

That realization took him by surprise, but he refused to dwell on what it could mean. He preferred to tell himself he simply needed some kind of closure where Jane was concerned. Either she would agree to come home with him and give their marriage a second chance, or she wouldn't.

One way or the other, she would also have to give him an explanation as to why she had left in the first place. If she had simply been unhappy, he would gladly vow to do whatever she asked to make it up to her. And if there was more to it than that, he would be open to any suggestions she had to offer. He wanted his wife back, and he wanted a *real* marriage, not the sham he had thought he needed almost eight months ago.

Max slept fitfully that night, troubled by strange

dreams he couldn't quite recall. Finally giving up on getting any rest, he arose well before dawn, dressed and left the apartment, taking care not to disturb Calvin.

The flight to San Antonio seemed interminable. He had brought along a briefcase full of paperwork, but he gave up on it within an hour. Instead, he alternately stared out the window and riffled though magazines, reading no more than a sentence or two here and there.

Once he was on the road in the car he had picked up at the San Antonio airport, some of his edginess eased. The sun shone brightly in the clear sky, throwing off heat that shimmered in waves above the asphalt highway. Unused to temperatures that climbed to the midnineties before noon, Max was thankful the car had tinted windows and an air conditioner that worked.

Once he got past the suburban sprawl of the city, traffic thinned appreciably. Following the winding roads that curved through the Texas hill country, Max's anticipation grew steadily. Soon now, very soon, he and Jane would be together again.

Serenity turned out to be larger than Max expected. Coming across a tourist information center near the downtown area, he stopped to get a street map of the town. With that and the address Frank Denny had given him, finding Emma Dalton's house was easy enough.

The charming, two-story, wood-frame cottage, freshly painted in shades of cream and dusky blue, surrounded by a low wooden fence and shaded by a huge old oak standing tall in a riotous garden full of flowers, sat back off the quiet, tree-lined street. Max parked at the curb, let himself into the yard through the little gate and walked up the narrow brick path to the long, shady porch. A wicker swing sporting brightly striped cushions rocked in a gentle breeze that carried the scent of herbs from the clay pots standing at attention along the railing.

Max rang the doorbell, then knocked on the heavy wooden door, but no one answered. Probably at work, he thought, glancing at his watch. It wasn't quite two o'clock yet.

Back in the car, he looked at the map again, located the library in the center of Serenity's business district and headed in that direction. He found a parking place on the street, fed coins into the meter, then walked into the old brick building.

Just inside the entryway, he paused, letting his eyes adjust to the dimness as he got his bearings. A huge room filled with bookcases opened off to his left, straight ahead a staircase led up to the second floor and to the right several doorways revealed what appeared to be business offices. Also to the right was a counter manned by an elderly woman with inquisitive eyes and a kindly smile.

"May I help you?" she asked.

"I'm...just looking," Max answered.

He didn't want to ask for Jane by name, and thus risk alerting her, unless he couldn't find her on his own.

"Certainly, sir. You're more than welcome. Take your time, and if you have any questions, one of our librarians will be happy to help you."

Max decided to start with the room to his left. Several women, obviously patrons, searched among the shelves marked Fiction. At a desk off to one side, a woman about Jane's age wearing wire-rimmed glasses ran her fingers through her mop of curly red hair as she glanced up at him. She smiled absentmindedly, then went back to the papers spread out in front of her.

Max eyed her consideringly, and after a few moments, she looked up at him again, her gaze suddenly wary. At the same time, Max heard a ripple of childish laughter filtering through an arched doorway on the opposite side of the room. As he turned toward the sound, he noted that the woman behind the desk was now standing.

"Sir? Can I help you?" she called out, her voice laced with authority.

Max didn't bother to reply as he strode toward the doorway, his heartbeat accelerating.

Inside the small room, a handful of preschoolers sprawled on the carpeted floor, their bright eyes fixed on the lovely young woman perched on a high stool, a picture book open on her lap.

Max's breath caught in his throat as he halted in the doorway, his gaze riveted to his wife. She seemed so different from the woman he had married almost five months ago.

Instead of the dark tailored business suits or classic pants and sweaters she had favored, she now wore a vibrant yellow, loose-fitting sundress that bared her tanned arms and swirled around her ankles. Her hair was swept up off her neck in a sassy ponytail held back with a flowered scarf tied in a floppy bow. Her cheeks bloomed with good health, her eyes sparkled with shared mischief and her mouth curved in an enchanting smile. She looked so happy, and so satisfied, sitting there, surrounded by children.

More than anything, Max wanted to wade through her tiny charges, sweep her into his arms and stake his claim. He ached to hold her close, to kiss her deeply and completely, then carry her off somewhere very private where he could strip off the baggy, oversize, yet incredibly sexy dress she wore and make mad, passionate love to her.

"'And then the itsy-bitsy purple monster began to grow and grow and...'" Jane read from the book, then looked up and met his gaze.

Her face paled, and her voice trailed away as something heartbreakingly akin to fear shadowed her eyes.

Of all the emotions Max had thought his arrival in Serenity would stir in his wife, fear most certainly hadn't been among them. Anger, perhaps, or joy, if he was very lucky. But not such obvious alarm.

"I'm sorry, sir. Our Thursday-afternoon story hour is for children five years old and under only."

The woman who had been sitting at the desk touched his arm, then gestured toward the larger room beyond.

Max glanced at her, then back at Jane. She looked dazed and confused now. Around her, the children sat wide-eyed, as well.

"Yes, of course," he murmured awkwardly. "I'll just...wait out here."

Turning away, he followed the woman's lead, but just outside the smaller room, he paused, determined not to go too far. Spying an empty chair along the wall nearby, he slumped into it, feeling more discouraged than he liked to admit, but not yet defeated.

Apparently assured that he would stay put, the woman—more than likely Jane's friend, Emma—returned to the room where Jane had stayed with the children, leaving him alone with his jumbled thoughts.

He could no longer assume that Jane had left him

simply because she was unhappy. There was much more to it than that. The look on her face when she first caught sight of him was all the proof he needed. But what had he done to frighten her so? For the life of him, he couldn't think of anything.

Maybe he should just leave her in peace. Hadn't that been what Calvin suggested he do? If she was afraid of him for some reason, maybe that *would* be the best—

"Max?"

At the sound of Jane's voice, he looked up and into her eyes, and knew that he wasn't going anywhere. At least, not just yet.

The fear was still there. But now, Max also saw what he wanted to believe was hope. For them, and the future they could have together?

Quite possibly, he thought with a measure of satisfaction, noting as Jane raised her hand and swiped at a wisp of hair trailing against her cheek that she still wore her wedding ring.

But there was only one way to find out for sure. Until he did, he had no intention of leaving Serenity, Texas.

offered to take over. Jane hesitated only a moment. The sooner she talked to Max, the sooner she'd be able to put her mind at ease.

She wanted to believe he had come to Serenity because he cared about her, and that if he cared about her, he might very well care about their baby, too. But she wouldn't know for sure until they'd had a chance to talk.

Jane saw Max sitting in the chair just outside the reading room, a bleak look on his face as he stared at the wood floor beneath his feet, and wanted to go to him, to kneel beside him and assure him everything would be all right. Instead, she stood silently for several seconds, eyeing him covertly.

His face had a gaunt look about it, as if he hadn't been eating or sleeping well, and he was dressed much more casually than she had ever seen him. The faded jeans and chambray shirt he wore not only added to his masculine appeal, but also made him seem approachable.

Love for him swelled in Jane's heart, and again the baby stirred in her womb. Finally finding the courage to speak his name, she announced her presence.

As Max looked up at her, his weariness seemed to fall away, replaced by a steely determination that had her stiffening her spine and straightening her shoulders. He stood, took a single step toward her, then halted when she, in turn, stepped back warily. She didn't dare let him get close enough to embrace her.

"I'm sorry," he muttered, his voice pitched low to suit their surroundings. "I didn't mean to alarm you."

"You didn't," she insisted. "Not really. I was just...surprised to see you."

"I got the feeling you were frightened, too. But

there's no reason to be. None at all. I didn't come here to cause you any grief. I've been concerned about you. I wanted to see you, talk to you, find out what happened.'' He hesitated, shoved his fingers through his hair. Then, his tone slightly accusing, he added, ''You just left without saying anything....''

''I tried to explain how I felt in my letter.''

''Yeah, I know. But if you'd told me face-to-face, maybe we could have worked things out.''

''Maybe,'' she agreed, then steered the conversation in a different direction as deftly as she could. ''I was wondering...how did you find me?''

''It wasn't easy.'' The barest hint of a wry smile tugged at the corners of his mouth. ''Since my butler and your lawyer refused to cooperate, I hired a private investigator.''

''You did?'' Jane stared at him in amazement, not quite sure what to think.

''Cost me a bundle, too,'' he added. His expression suddenly serious again, he took another step toward her. ''But it was worth every penny.''

''It was?''

Mesmerized by the gleam of sincerity in his pale gray eyes, Jane forgot to move away as he closed what remained of the distance between them.

''Yes.'' Ever so gently, as if afraid he would startle her, he reached out and brushed his fingers against her cheek. ''God, Janie, I've missed you.''

''Oh, Max...'' Making a desperate attempt to gather her wits about her, Jane lifted her chin and squared her shoulders. ''I never meant to cause you any upset. I honestly believed you'd be glad to find me gone. Since you seemed as...dissatisfied with our marriage as I was, there didn't seem to be any reason for us to stay together. I thought bowing out gracefully would be the simplest solution.''

She knew she wasn't telling him the whole truth, but she wasn't ready to say anything about the baby yet. While he obviously had some feelings for her, she wasn't sure how deep they were, or how reliable.

He was a powerful man, used to getting what he wanted, and in a way, she had thwarted him. Coming after her and winning her back might be nothing more to him than a test of wills he intended to prove himself best at.

As if sensing her resistance, Max didn't crowd her. He gazed at her thoughtfully for a long moment, then tucked his hands in the pockets of his jeans and nodded toward the small group of women gathering on the opposite side of the reading room doorway.

''Is there someplace a little more private where we can talk?''

Jane glanced at the mothers—all eyeing her and Max with avid curiosity—then at her watch. Story hour would be over in about five minutes. Fifteen minutes after that, she was scheduled to lead a group of older children, all members of the summer book club, in a discussion of the diary of Anne Frank.

Of course, Emma would cover for her. But Jane wasn't really all that eager to go off on her own with Max just yet. She wanted a little time to herself. Time to calm down a bit so she could better judge what his true intentions were. Then she could weigh her options more reasonably before she decided on a course of action.

Once she told Max about the baby, there would be no going back. She would have to live with the consequences whether they turned out to be good or bad. In her heart, she knew Max had a right to know she was carrying his child. But she could still remember how adamantly against having children he'd been just eight months ago.

What were the odds that he would change his mind once he knew about her pregnancy? Never much of a gambler, Jane wasn't quite ready to find out.

"I have to work until four-thirty," she told him, adding what she hoped was just the right amount of regret to her tone.

"Fine." He nodded agreeably. "I'll find a place to wait."

"Why don't you come to dinner at Emma's house instead? Say around six o'clock," Jane suggested, thinking quickly.

She didn't want him hanging around the library for the rest of the afternoon. She'd end up a nervous wreck. At Emma's house, she would find it easier to keep him at arm's length with her friend around to act as a buffer.

Max frowned and shifted restlessly, seeming less than pleased with her plan.

"I'd really like some time alone with..." he began, only to be cut off by the children boisterously spilling out of the reading room.

Emma tried to shush them without much success. Then, as the women and children drifted away, she moved to stand beside Jane. Though barely five feet two inches tall, there was a protectively proprietary air about her as she put a hand on Jane's arm.

"Everything all right?"

"Yes, just fine," Jane assured her. "Let me introduce you. This is Maxwell Hamilton. Max, my dear friend, Emma Dalton.''

"Mr. Hamilton."

"Ms. Dalton."

Jane hid a smile as they eyed each other suspiciously.

"I hope you don't mind that I've invited Max to dinner tonight."

"Oh, no, not at all," Emma assured her.

"So, you'll be there at six?" Jane risked a glance at Max.

Obviously aware that he'd be fighting a losing battle by trying to go up against the two of them, he nodded in agreement.

"Yeah, sure."

"Jane has another group coming in any minute now," Emma advised. "Why don't you come with me so I can give you directions to the house?"

"I already know the way to your house," he stated simply.

"Well, then, I guess we'll see you there."

"Unless my wife decides to run off again in the meantime."

Though Max spoke to Emma, he glanced at Jane questioningly.

"I'm not going anywhere, Max. I promise."

"Good."

Before Jane realized what Max had in mind, he bent toward her, and without touching her anywhere else, brushed a feathery kiss against her lips. The contact lasted no more than a moment or two. But there was heat in it—a heat that seared through to her very soul as he teased her lower lip with the tip of his tongue.

Jane's breath caught in her throat, and she had to clench her hands to keep from reaching for him.

Evidently pleased with whatever he saw in her startled expression, Max smiled slowly, turned on his heel and walked away.

As Jane watched him disappear among the bookshelves, the baby rolled and tumbled inside her yet again—this time more forcefully than ever. Her thoughts whirling, she put a hand over her tummy, seeking comfort from the tactile connection.

Ah, little one, your daddy's making me crazy....

"So *that* is Maxwell Hamilton," Emma mused. "The man you say married you only as a matter of convenience. Looks to me like he's ready to make amends, dear friend."

"Do you really think so?" The heat of a blush warmed Jane's cheeks as she met Emma's gaze.

"Oh, yes, I do. You should see the way he looks at you, and that kiss..." Emma waved her hand as if she'd touched something hot.

Though Jane laughed and shook her head, she was inordinately pleased with her friend's assessment.

"Do you think he knows about the baby?"

"He hasn't mentioned it yet, and I'm fairly sure he would have if he did."

"Are you going to tell him tonight?"

"I'm still trying to decide."

"Ah, that explains the dinner invitation. Well, count on me to run interference as long as you as want."

"Thanks, Em." Jane hugged her friend gratefully.

"There's no need to rush into anything unless you're sure."

"No, there isn't," Jane agreed, rubbing her hand

over her tummy as she stared wistfully off into the distance.

More than anything, she wanted to believe Max's determination to find her boded well for the future. One small but highly significant obstacle remained to their living happily ever after, though.

Until she told Max about the baby, she couldn't allow herself to get her hopes up. She had already suffered enough disappointment to last a lifetime. She wasn't about to set herself up, only to get knocked down again.

No matter how much she wanted to believe in him.

Chapter Eleven

"Hamilton residence."

"Calvin, it's me…Max."

Standing in a blazing-hot telephone booth on the sidewalk outside the library, Max squinted against the bright sunlight that glared through the glass. So pleased was he by how well his initial encounter with Jane had gone, he hadn't wasted any time calling the butler to let him know what was happening. Preparations would have to be made for their homecoming, and he owed Calvin as much advance notice as possible.

"You left awfully early this morning, sir. Had I known of your plans, I could have had breakfast ready for you," the butler chastised mildly.

"I had an early flight out," Max admitted, still vaguely discomfited by his duplicity. "I didn't want to disturb you."

"I don't recall your mentioning any out-of-town business on today's schedule."

"This came up rather suddenly."

"Ah, I see," Calvin murmured. "You're being very secretive, Max. May I ask where you are and when I can expect you home again, or would that be out of line?"

"I'm in Serenity, Texas, and you can expect *us* home Sunday at the latest," Max replied, bracing himself for the possibility of a tirade.

The silence emanating from the other end of the telephone line took him by surprise.

"Still there, Calvin?" he prodded after several moments.

"Yes, of course."

"Surprised you, huh?"

"You could say that," Calvin answered cautiously.

Max frowned as he wiped a trickle of sweat from the side of his face with the back of his wrist.

"You don't sound very happy."

"I take it you've seen Mrs. Hamilton? How is she? In good health?"

"She's just fine. At least as far as I could tell." Max's frown deepened. "Why? Has she been ill?"

"No, not...ill. Not that I know of."

"Well, she seemed perfectly all right to me."

"Was she...glad to see you?"

"After the initial shock wore off, yes, I think she was."

"Where is she now? There with you?"

"No, she's working at the library until four-thirty. But I'm having dinner with her and her friend Emma this evening."

"I see." Calvin paused, then added hesitantly, "Max, why did you go there?"

"Jane is my wife. I want her back," Max stated succinctly.

"Under any circumstances?" the butler prodded. "Any circumstances at all?"

"What the hell is that supposed to mean?" Max growled, something about the way Calvin had worded his question making him oddly uneasy.

"You had certain expectations of the kind of marriage you wanted—"

"I know," Max cut in. "I was wrong. I admit it. I caused whatever problems there are between us, but I think we can work them out. We've got so much going for us. Basically, we're quite compatible. I saw that from the very beginning. But after Alyssa, I was afraid of getting emotionally involved."

"And now you're not?"

"Now I'm not," Max admitted.

"What if she wants more?"

"More? What more could she possibly want than a happy marriage and a satisfying career? I can guarantee she'll have both those things along with the financial security I can provide for her. Hell, she doesn't even have to work anymore if she doesn't want to. She could spend a few days a week volunteering at the library. She's doing that here, and from what I could see, she seemed to be enjoying it. I could take more time off, too. We could do some traveling together, maybe buy a summer home on one of the islands."

"Sounds like a nice life, Max. But what if that's not exactly what *she* has in mind?"

"You know, I'm getting the distinct impression

there's something you're trying to tell me. Why don't you just spit it out?'' Max said, his patience wearing thin.

''Just don't rush to any conclusions, Max. Especially tonight when you and Jane are together. Try not to say or do anything rash. Anything you might end up regretting once you've had time to…reconsider.''

''Jeez, Calvin, I'm not a total moron.''

''I realize that, sir. But we all have moments when we're caught off guard, and sometimes we forget ourselves,'' the butler cautioned.

Max knew that was true. But he couldn't imagine anything he might say to his wife tonight that would cause him remorse. Now that he had found Jane, his only intention was to woo her into his arms.

''I'll try to keep that in mind,'' he conceded after a moment.

''Very good, sir,'' Calvin acknowledged. Then, his tone suddenly brisk and businesslike, he continued in another vein. ''You said something about returning by Sunday at the latest?''

''Unless Jane needs more time to settle her affairs here. I'll let you know tomorrow. In the meantime, I'd like you to start getting the apartment ready for our return.''

''Shall I arrange to have her things moved into the spare bedroom again?''

''I don't think that will be necessary. I'd rather you order a change of bed linens for the master suite— something a little less austere. Call the decorator we've used in the past and give her an idea of what Jane might like. Fresh flowers would be a nice touch, too. Plan to serve dinner out on the balcony Sunday night, as well. Weather permitting, of course.''

"Of course," Calvin agreed. "I'll take care of everything."

"I knew I could count on you," Max replied, ignoring the tiny thread of worry still underlying the butler's tone.

There was no reason for him to be concerned. But Max hadn't the time to convince him of it.

"Always, sir."

"Any calls for me?"

"None."

"Well, then, I'll talk to you again tomorrow."

"I'll be looking forward to it," the butler assured him solemnly.

Max had expected Calvin to be more pleased that he had gone after Jane than he seemed. But he saw no reason to dwell on what might be causing the man to be so reticent. Calvin had never been one to beat around the bush, but maybe the strained relationship they'd endured over the past several weeks had made him more cautious about blurting out just anything.

After feeding more coins into the parking meter, Max checked in with Ada, as well as with his various department heads. He had learned long ago to hire people he could trust implicitly, then delegate as much work as possible. That way, Hamilton Enterprises ran smoothly regardless of where he happened to be. Just as he found it had so far that day.

His calls to the office complete, Max walked the short distance to the tourist information center, scanned a listing of accommodations and finally chose a cozy-sounding bed-and-breakfast on a side street just a couple of blocks from Emma Dalton's house. With another telephone call, he secured the largest room available—actually a suite that occupied the house's entire third floor—for three nights. Just to be on the safe side, he told himself.

That done, he returned to his car, stopping first in a little shop to buy a bottle of wine, then at an old-fashioned German bakery, where he selected a truly luscious-looking chocolate confection. With luck, one or the other would smooth his way with the inimitable Ms. Dalton. She hadn't looked to be one to brook any nonsense. Having her on his side couldn't hurt.

As for Jane...

Max had something very special for her. Something he had wanted to return to her for months now.

The bed-and-breakfast turned out to be just as charming as he'd hoped. It was also spotlessly clean, and after the heat outdoors, refreshingly cool. Best of all, he seemed to be the only guest staying there.

Once he'd checked in, he took a shower and changed into fresh clothes. Then he dug through his carry-on bag and found the flat black velvet box. He removed the diamond bracelet and tucked it into his pants pocket.

Tonight he was going to propose to Jane all over again—the way he should have done eight months ago. And when he fastened the bracelet around her wrist this time, there wouldn't be any doubt in her mind why he wanted her to have it.

Aware that it was almost six o'clock, Max retrieved the bottle of wine and the bakery box, then left his room. Outside, the temperature still seemed high, but he preferred to walk the short distance to Emma's house rather than drive.

Once darkness had fallen, the air would cool, making the walk back a much more pleasurable interlude. Especially with Jane by his side.

Chapter Twelve

"How do I look?" Jane asked, pivoting in front of Emma so her pale pink, sleeveless sundress flared about her calves.

It was similar in style to the one she'd worn earlier, with a high collar edged in white eyelet and tiny pearl buttons halfway down the bodice—to draw the eye upward as all the maternity magazines suggested. She had pinned her hair in a loose knot atop her head, as well, then added a pair of dangling gold-and-pearl earrings that shivered delicately against her neck whenever she moved.

"As lovely as ever," Emma replied.

"I wasn't fishing for a compliment," Jane commented in a dry tone.

"What, then?"

"Do I *look* pregnant?"

"Hmm, let me think...." Emma teased. "As I seem

to recall, a few days ago you would have been thrilled to hear me say yes, but now—''

''Emma, *please*...''

''No, you do not look pregnant. Except when you put those protective hands of yours on your tummy. I know it's instinctive, but the way you do it, only a blind man wouldn't realize—''

The pealing of the front doorbell cut off the last of Emma's admonition.

''Oh, no. He's here,'' Jane murmured.

''Right on time,'' Emma said, glancing at her watch.

''I'm not sure I'm ready to face him again.''

''Then go in the kitchen and toss the salad while I get the door.''

Jane didn't need any additional urging. Whatever happened between her and Max tonight, her entire future hung in the balance. She knew what she wanted the outcome to be, but she also knew the odds weren't necessarily in her favor.

She had called Calvin just as soon as she and Emma got home from the library, and while her conversation with him had been somewhat reassuring, she still had some reason to be concerned. The butler had been fairly sure Max wasn't aware of her condition, so her secret was safe for the time being. But Calvin had also warned her that Max was intent on wooing her into returning to Seattle with him. She could never allow herself to do that without telling him everything first.

Much as she hated to admit it, Jane knew she was caught between a rock and a hard place. The moment she'd looked up to see Max at the library that afternoon, her defenses had started to crumble. She hadn't been able to send him away then. How could she possibly do it now? She wasn't strong enough to stand up to him. Not when she cared for him too deeply to hold him at arm's length.

Which meant she had no choice but to tell him about the baby. Otherwise, she would be playing games with him—something she had no right to do.

At least she wouldn't have to bear much longer the weight of anxiety that had pressed upon her since Max had walked into her life again, Jane reminded herself as she took the salad dressing from the refrigerator. Though it wasn't quite the bright side she would have wished for, she had to admit it was better than nothing.

She barely had time to add the dressing to the chopped greens and veggies in the glass bowl on the kitchen counter when Emma breezed through the doorway. Max followed, looking more like the man she'd married than he had that afternoon.

He was dressed in pleated khaki slacks and a white dress shirt with the sleeves rolled back a couple of turns in deference to the summer heat. In one hand he carried a bottle of red wine, and in the other a bakery box.

There was also a definite spring in his step, as well as a devilishly masculine glint in his eyes that sent a shiver of anticipation racing down Jane's spine the moment she met his gaze. Even had she not been warned, she would have known what he had in mind. Seduction, plain and simple. *Her* seduction...

"Look, Jane, our gentleman caller has arrived bearing gifts," Emma chirped gaily, taking the wine bottle and bakery box Max offered her as he paused by the counter. She set the wine aside, then focused her attention on the box, loosening the tape that held the top flap down and peeking inside. ''Oh, yum. Chocolate decadence. My favorite.''

''Your's, too, I hope,'' Max said, his gaze still holding Jane's.

''Yes, mine, too,'' she assured him, blushing as she turned away.

Her hands trembling slightly, she reached for the oversize wooden fork and spoon, and began to toss the salad fixings with Emma's homemade herb dressing.

''I think the lasagna's just about ready,'' Emma announced. Bustling over to the oven, she added, ''It's one of Jane's specialties, made with spinach, feta cheese and a cream sauce that's to die for.''

''Smells delicious,'' Max murmured as he slid his hands in his pockets.

From the corner of her eye, Jane saw him watching her intently. Though she willed herself to take slow, steady breaths, her face warmed even more. What must he be thinking? she wondered, then realized she was probably better off not knowing.

''I thought we'd eat in here,'' Emma burbled on, indicating the table set for three tucked in an alcove surrounded by a bay window that looked out over the flower-filled backyard. ''Max, why don't you open the wine while I find some glasses? And Jane, you can go ahead and serve the salad.''

The meal progressed as well as could have been expected under the circumstances. The only glitch came when Jane refused a glass of wine. Max eyed her curiously. The vintage he'd chosen was one he knew to be among her favorites. She made a comment about alcohol not agreeing with her when the weather was hot and thankfully he seemed satisfied.

Emma's presence also served as a buffer between

her and Max. Her friend kept the conversation light and impersonal, quickly filling any gaps with amusing anecdotes about small-town life in general or the library in particular. Jane went along with her gladly, as did Max.

But something in his expression every time she met his gaze warned that her reprieve wasn't going to last much longer. In deference to Emma, he was minding his manners, but Jane knew that sooner or later he would find a way to get her all to himself. Then she would have to answer the questions he would inevitably ask.

Ignoring Emma's efforts to shoo him into the living room, Max lent a hand with the tidying up after they finished their coffee and dessert. In fact, he was rather insistent about helping out, revealing his ulterior motive only as Emma stowed the last dish in the dishwasher. At that moment, he took Jane by the arm and whisked her toward the back door in a deft move she admired in spite of herself.

"Why don't you show me Emma's garden before it gets dark?" he suggested as he reached for the knob.

Dear friend that she was, Emma moved forward to intervene, but Jane glanced her way and gave a negative shake of her head. She had put Max off long enough.

"I was just about to suggest that myself," she replied, inhaling the warm, fragrant, early-evening air as she led the way outside.

The sun had only just begun to dip behind the trees, but the heat of the day had passed and the garden was already awash in deepening shadow. Slowly, Jane wandered along the narrow brick path that wove among the riotous beds of brightly colored flowers, heading toward the gazebo perched in one corner at the far end of the yard. Max walked along beside her, his hands in his pockets, his arm brushing hers companionably every now and then.

"I like your friend Emma. She's very nice. I can understand why you came here," he said after a while, his voice pitched low.

"She's been a good friend to me for a long time now," Jane replied.

"You grew up together here in Serenity?"

"Not exactly," she hedged.

"How did you meet, then?"

Max had never seemed all that interested in her past, but that had suited her just fine. Talking about the strange twists of fate she'd endured as a young girl had never been easy for her. Now, oddly enough, she found herself welcoming the opportunity.

Anything to buy a little more time, she thought with a wry smile.

"I spent the first ten years of my life in San Antonio. I was the pampered only child of seemingly wealthy parents. When they were killed in an automobile accident, it was discovered they were deeply in debt. Since they had no close relatives—at least none willing to take in a destitute child—I was placed with a foster family.

"The conditions there weren't especially good. We just weren't...compatible. Shortly after my thirteenth birthday, I was moved to another home here in Serenity.

"Emma was already living there along with two other girls. We were all about the same age, and all pretty much alone in the world. The four of us became friends, as well as foster sisters. After graduating from high school, we all went our separate ways, but thanks to Emma's efforts, we've always managed to keep in touch, and we've always known we could count on each other in an emergency.''

''Sounds like you were happy here.''

''As happy as I could be under the circumstances.''

''Happier than you were in Seattle?''

''No, Max. I've never been happier than I was in Seattle,'' she admitted.

''Until I came along and mucked things up,'' he muttered darkly.

Jane risked a glance at him, then quickly looked away again. He seemed angry with himself, but there was no need for him to be. He had looked out for his best interests, and in her own way, so had she.

''I knew what I was getting into when I accepted your proposal,'' she stated simply. ''You certainly didn't lure me with false promises. You told me what you wanted, and at the time, I was sure that was what I wanted, too.''

''Why, Jane?'' he asked, obviously bewildered. ''Why did you feel you had to settle for that kind of relationship? You're an attractive, intelligent woman.''

She hesitated a long moment, debating about how honest she should be. She could hedge a bit to save face, but she didn't really want any lies between them. Not after tonight. Any relationship they had in the future would have to be based on honesty. Love wouldn't have a chance otherwise.

''I was sexually abused by my first foster father. Not raped outright, but...handled in...ugly ways. It went on for almost three years. After that, the thought of having sex was...distasteful. Dating was out of the question, and I certainly couldn't see myself entering into a traditional marriage.

"But I was so lonely. I wanted, *needed,* something more in my life. Then you offered me the kind of companionship I never thought I would have with a man."

"But that wasn't what you got, was it?" he asked, taking her by the arm and turning her to face him as they halted near the gazebo. "I didn't even begin to hold up my end of the bargain, did I? Instead, I really made a mess of things."

Jane shrugged helplessly, then eased away from him and started up the short flight of steps. He had, but not in the way he meant.

There was a narrow bench circling the interior wall of the gazebo, but she chose not to sit. Instead, she leaned against one of the support posts and stared at the house, brightened by the soft glow of lamplight filtering through the windows. Max followed, halting right behind her, and put his hands on her shoulders.

"Why did you follow me here?" she asked, the rhythm of her heartbeat accelerating.

"Because you mean a lot to me, Janie. More than I ever let you know, and for that, I am deeply sorry. I thought I knew what I wanted, what I needed, in a relationship until you left me. Then I realized what a fool I'd been, turning away from you and all you'd been trying to offer me.

"On our wedding night, when we made love...the way you made me feel...it scared me. So much, I tried to fight it. And all I really succeeded in doing was driving you away."

"I couldn't go on the way we were, Max. Feeling that you could barely tolerate my presence. We weren't even friends anymore. Just strangers being polite to each other whenever our paths happened to cross. I thought the kind of marriage you proposed would be better than nothing, but we didn't even have that.''

"I know, and I'm sorry. I really let you down. But I want to make it up to you, if only you'll give me the chance. We can be friends and lovers,'' he vowed, feathering the lightest of kisses along the nape of her neck. "Tell me it's not too late for that. Please, Janie…''

"Oh, Max,'' she murmured, her insides melting as his teeth nibbled teasingly along her earlobe. "It's not that simple.''

"Can you honestly say you don't have any feelings for me anymore?'' he growled as he turned her toward him and tipped her face up, forcing her to meet his searching gaze.

He was saying all the things she had longed to hear. His words were filled with promises for the future. But sadly, he assumed that future would only include the two of them.

"I care for you deeply, Max. I have almost from the very start,'' she admitted. "That's why I made love with you. But it's how you feel about me that matters most now. You set certain…parameters when you asked me to marry you, and I agreed to abide by them. But now you want some of those parameters to change—''

"And you don't?'' he cut in.

"Oh, no. I *do*. But…''

"Are you worried that I'll change my mind again?'' he asked, stroking her cheek with his fingertips. "I won't. I swear it.''

"No, I—"

"I swear it," Max repeated.

Giving her no chance to reply, he bent his head and kissed her so passionately that shock waves rippled through her. Her head spun, and her heart hammered as he claimed her mouth with a fierceness that would have terrified her in the past, his tongue plundering possessively.

In some tiny corner of her mind, Jane knew she should stop him. There was still too much left unsaid between them. Yet she clung to him, her fingers gripping the fabric of his shirt, giving herself up to the pleasure he offered her—a pleasure she had never thought to experience again.

"Come with me, Jane. Come with me now, and I'll show you just how much you mean to me," he growled.

"I can't, Max. Not yet," she said. "I have to…have to…"

"All you have to do is let me make things right between us," he assured her. "Trust me. The rest will come."

Trust him…

That was what Jane had done on her wedding night, and what she wanted to do again now. Never before had she allowed a man so close. Not once, much less twice. Nor had she ever entrusted her fate to anyone as she was tempted to do with Max.

But soon now, he would pull her closer, put his hands on her body, sense the changes and realize—

He toyed with her ear again, licking at it, then tugging at the lobe with his teeth in a way that made her ache. She sighed, her thoughts scattering, and gave herself up to his tender ministrations.

Laughing softly, triumphantly, Max urged her closer as he took her mouth again. His hands roved over her shoulders, then down her upper arms, his thumbs grazing the sides of her hypersensitive breasts.

Gasping and shivering, Jane arched into his touch. Still kissing her hungrily, Max cupped her breasts in his palms and fingered her nipples through the fabric of her clothing.

Unable to stop herself, Jane whimpered softly, the pleasure pulsing through her almost more than she could bear. Her legs trembled so, she had to cling to him to keep from sinking to her knees.

Max laughed again as he nuzzled her neck.

"You feel so good," he muttered. "So damned good…"

Lost in a whirl of erotic sensations, Jane couldn't seem to keep track of Max's clever hands. Too late, she realized they were sliding along her rib cage, then down lower until his left had rested on her bottom and his right hand stroked over her belly.

"What's this?" he murmured, his breath warm against her neck, a hint of amusement in his voice.

He splayed his fingers over her and rubbed his hand back and forth, as if trying to measure the unexpected changes he'd detected in her lower body.

Unable to speak, Jane went still, hardly daring to breathe.

Suddenly, Max tensed, his hand still curved over her belly. Slowly, he lifted his head, and in the twilight Jane saw the wonderment in his eyes as his hand tightened over her protectively. She started to smile as relief flooded through her. But then, the look on his face changed.

"You're pregnant, aren't you?" he asked, his voice flat.

Not as much a question as a bald statement uttered without any emotion at all.

"Yes," she whispered, her smile fading.

His lips twisted grimly as he drew his hands away and took a step back.

"Max, please…" she began, then bit off the rest of her plea.

She would not beg him for anything…ever.

Saying nothing, he backed even farther from her, stumbled on the steps, then caught himself on the railing. He wavered there for what seemed like an eternity, an odd mix of emotions playing across his features. He seemed not only angry, but afraid.

Hurt and confused, Jane stared at him silently.

Finally, a panicked look in his eyes, Max turned away from her. He bolted down the steps, then fled across the garden without a backward glance, his footsteps echoing loudly in the quiet of the night.

Jane watched him go, quelling the urge to call out to him, to beg him not to leave her. She absolutely refused to swallow what little pride she had left.

As she heard the back door of Emma's house open, then close, she sank onto the wooden bench. Tears stung her eyes, tears she tried hard not to shed. He wasn't worth crying over. No man was. But he had crushed the last of her hopes and dreams with a finality she couldn't deny.

She should have been prepared for it, she chastised herself, then remembered that she had been until he'd taken her in his arms and asked for her trust. Like a fool, she had given it, just as she had on her wedding night. And now, as then, he had thrown it back in her face.

Never again, she vowed, as a sob welled in her chest. Never, *ever,* again…

Covering her face with her hands, she began to weep, unable to contain the wretchedness lodged in her heart any longer.

"Oh, Jane, what's happened?" Emma crooned.

Seeming to materialize out of nowhere, she sat on the bench and gathered Jane into her arms, and she leaned against her gratefully.

"He…he finally realized I was…I was pregnant," she said, her tears falling even harder as all the years of stoically facing one disappointment after another weighed upon her, a burden she could no longer bear with dispassion.

"I was afraid that might be it," Emma murmured, stroking Jane's hair and rocking her gently.

After what seemed like a very long time, Jane's tears finally began to abate. Not only had she indulged herself more than seemed necessary, but also the roller coaster ride of emotions she'd endured over the past few hours couldn't be good for the baby.

Gratefully, she accepted the tissues Emma pressed into her hand, mopped her face and blew her nose.

"Better?" Emma asked.

"Not really," Jane admitted, her voice quavering.

"It might not be much consolation, but he looked like he was in a state of shock when he stormed through the house and out the front door. I tried to stop him, but I don't think he saw me, much less heard a word I said."

"Couldn't get away fast enough, could he?" Jane muttered sarcastically.

"Did he say anything at all about the baby?"

"Aside from 'You're pregnant,' not a word. He just stared at me as if I were something nasty smeared on the sidewalk, then he walked away."

"Oh, Jane, I'm so sorry. I never should have let him get you alone out here. But I honestly didn't believe he would react that way."

"There's no need for you to apologize, Emma. What happened wasn't your fault. I should have been expecting it. Actually, I *was* until he started talking about trusting him to make things right between us. He said he didn't want children, but I didn't want to believe he meant it. That was my mistake."

"So now what?" Emma asked.

"Now I pick up where I left off this afternoon, a little wiser, if nothing else," Jane answered philosophically.

"And Max? He's out of the picture completely?"

"Oh, yes, Max is most definitely out of the picture. In fact, he can go to the devil for all I care. We don't need him. Do we, little one?" Jane stroked her tummy tenderly, and as if sensing her need for positive reinforcement, the baby moved reassuringly.

They were going to be just fine on their own, Jane told herself, and that was all that really mattered to her now.

Chapter Thirteen

Max had no idea how long he wandered the quiet streets of Serenity after he left Emma Dalton's house. Nor could he have said how he finally found his way back to the bed-and-breakfast where he had planned to spend the weekend. He walked aimlessly, his hurried footsteps eating up one patch of pavement after another, aware of little more than the heartrending memories that replayed over and over in his mind.

In devastating detail, he saw Alyssa lying on the delivery table, struggling weakly, gasping for breath, beseeching him with her eyes as the monitors beeped wildly and the lifeblood drained from her body. Then, in a whirl of confusion, it was Jane he saw reaching out to him, begging for his help.

Silently, Max keened with a rage and pain so vital it nearly knocked him to his knees.

How could fate have played such a cruel trick on

him? He had finally found the courage to admit how much Jane meant to him. And now he had to face the possibility that what had happened to Alyssa that awful night eight years ago could very well happen to her, as well.

He couldn't go through that agony again. Couldn't stand by and watch as death claimed his beloved at the very moment they should have been celebrating new life.

Of course, he had only himself to blame. If he'd had sense enough to keep his wits about him on his wedding night, he wouldn't have found himself in such a terrifying predicament. Instead, he had thrown caution to the wind, taking what he'd wanted without any thought to the consequences.

He had led Jane to believe sex wouldn't be an issue, so she'd had no reason to protect herself from pregnancy. And he had been too wrapped up in the moment to take the necessary precautions himself. Now she was the one who had to pay the price.

And if the final accounting included *her* precious life as it had Alyssa's?

Max didn't think he had the strength or the courage to face that kind of tragedy again.

So you're going to abandon her without a backward glance? his conscience prodded. Going to walk away from her...no, run away, and leave her to cope alone?

Jane was carrying *his* child. The child he had planted in her womb with a passion that had overridden every ounce of common sense he had ever possessed. The child she could have had aborted, but hadn't.

How easily she could have done that without his even knowing. A relatively simple procedure, and she could have gone on with the insouciant life she'd been leading. She'd had every right. The pregnancy hadn't been her doing. Nor had it been something she'd bargained for.

Yet Jane had willingly allowed the baby to turn her life upside down while doing everything in her power to relieve *him* of what she had apparently believed he'd consider an unwanted burden.

Bravely, she had set off on her own, freeing him as best she knew how of any obligation he might feel toward her. She had asked for nothing from him but the freedom to bear his child in peace. And he hadn't even been able to allow her that small concession.

He had come after her, determined to win her back. He had led her on with words of love, only to run from her like a man possessed when she looked at him, her heart in her eyes, begging him silently to share her wonder and joy at the life they had created.

Remembering what he had done to Jane—the hope he had stirred in her, then cruelly dashed—Max sank down on the porch steps of the bed-and-breakfast and buried his head in his hands. He could imagine only too well how badly he had hurt her, and he hated himself for it.

She was his wife, the mother of his child, a child she obviously wanted more than anything in life. She deserved so much better from him. But he had nothing left to give her. Nothing that wouldn't cost him dearly if he lost her as he'd lost Alyssa.

The best thing he could do—for her sake, as well as his own—was to leave her in peace just as Calvin had suggested two months ago.

Of course, he would provide for her and the baby financially. He could guarantee they would never want for anything, and he would. He would also arrange for a divorce as quickly as possible. Once that was final, he should be able to bury whatever remained of his feelings for her. He could immerse himself in his work and get on with his life. His *solitary* life…

Fully intending to leave for Seattle first thing in the morning, Max let himself into the house with the key he'd been given and climbed the stairs to his room. To his relief, he met no one along the way. Evidently, his hosts as well as any other guests who'd arrived that evening had already retired, too.

Overcome with exhaustion, he fell into bed, but sleep came only in snatches filled with vaguely nightmarish visions. Just after dawn, he awoke with a start, the sound of Jane's voice ringing in his ears. In his dream, she had been lying alone on the dirty floor of a run-down room, blood smearing her legs as she wept helplessly.

Scrubbing a hand over his face, Max admitted that he couldn't leave Jane in Serenity, after all. One way or another, she had to come back to Seattle with him. At least there, she would get the best care money could buy. And he would be able to keep an eye on her, as well.

He knew better than to think convincing her to go along with his plan would be easy. Not after the way he had behaved the night before. But he was sure that eventually he would be able to make her see reason. She might put up some resistance at the outset. Still, she was a sensible woman. In the end, she would do what she knew was best for her baby.

Max joined the other guests—a young couple and two elderly women—for breakfast in the home's glass-walled sunroom. Preferring not to socialize, he sat alone at a small table overlooking a garden that paled in comparison to Emma Dalton's, and read a copy of the *Houston Chronicle* as he sipped dark-roast coffee and munched on a homemade blueberry muffin.

He lingered longer than the others, telling himself he didn't want to arrive at Emma's house too early on a Saturday morning. In fact, he was actually trying to work up the nerve to show his face there again.

Max knew better than to expect a warm welcome. But when Emma answered the front door and saw him standing on her porch, he was surprised that the look on her face didn't turn him to stone.

"Yes?" she inquired curtly as she eyed him through the wire mesh of the screen door.

"I'd like to see Jane, please," he replied.

"I'm not sure that's going to be possible."

Max's gut clenched as all sorts of frightening possibilities crowded into his mind.

"She's all right, isn't she?" he demanded.

"As *all right* as can be expected under the circumstances," she retorted.

"Look, I know I went off half-cocked last night, but I've come to make amends."

"Well, I'm sure that bit of news will have her jumping for joy."

"Only if you deliver it," Max growled, unable to contain his frustration.

Difficult as it had been for him to do, he'd admitted that he'd made a mistake. He didn't appreciate having his nose rubbed in it by a sassy redhead.

"I'd warn you not to hold your breath, but I'd just love to come back and find you turning blue," she drawled.

Without awaiting a reply, Emma shut the door in

Max's face. He stood where he was, hands in his pockets, inhaling the herb-scented summer air for several minutes. Finally, too restless to stay still any longer, he began to pace along the length of the porch.

What the hell was taking so long? Had Emma actually told Jane that he wanted to talk to her? Or had the woman taken it upon herself to protect her from the ogre she'd had the misfortune to marry? He certainly wouldn't put that past her.

There was also a chance the two of them had decided to let him cool his heels while they disappeared through the back garden. But surely they couldn't think that would divert him for long.

Max was about to jab his finger into the bell button again when the door swung open slowly. Jane peered at him hesitantly, not quite meeting his gaze. After a moment, she glanced over her shoulder, said something he couldn't quite hear, then came out onto the porch, leaving the inner door slightly ajar.

"You wanted to see me?" she asked without any hint of interest or enthusiasm.

She wore a pair of navy blue knit shorts and a bright green oversize T-shirt that didn't hide her pregnancy quite as well as the dresses had. Her dark hair hung about her shoulders in a tumbled mess, and her face, devoid of makeup, seemed unnaturally pale. There was a bruised look about her eyes, as well.

Yesterday she had sparkled with vitality. Today all the life seemed to have drained out of her. Studying her surreptitiously, Max was reminded of how she'd looked just before she'd left Seattle. Though she stood straight and tall, her chin tipped at a defiant angle, there was something waiflike about her.

He wanted to gather her into his arms, hold her

close and kiss her sadness away. But he had given up that privilege when he'd walked away from her last night.

"We need to talk," he said, then gestured toward the porch swing. "Why don't we sit down?"

"I don't think that's really necessary," she countered.

"What I have to say may take some time."

"Your actions last night spoke louder than any words possibly could, Max. I can't imagine what you might have to add that would be of any importance to me now."

For the first time since Jane had joined him on the porch, she met his gaze directly. The anguish he saw in her eyes made him flinch.

"Just hear me out, please," he begged, reaching out to touch her cheek. "I know I behaved badly last night—"

She jerked away from his hand as if she'd been burned.

"You let your true feelings be known. There's nothing wrong with that."

"You don't understand—" he began, then caught himself.

How could he explain his actions without revealing the horrifying details of Alyssa's death? That wasn't something to which he could subject her. Not when she would be facing her own labor and delivery within a few short months.

"Oh, I think I do," she said. "My getting pregnant was an accident. One I welcomed even though I knew you wouldn't. I wanted to keep the baby, but I didn't feel it was right to make you feel responsible. That's why I left Seattle."

"But I *am* responsible, Jane."

"Technically, yes." With a weary shrug, she turned and crossed to the swing. "Maybe 'obligated' is a better way of putting it. I didn't want you to feel *obligated,* Max."

"You're my wife. You're carrying my child—"

"So file for divorce and allow me to have sole custody. Then you'll be off the hook."

"No," he responded, surprised by the vehemence in his voice.

"Oh, Max..." Jane sighed and shook her head as she looked out across the lawn. "Don't be pigheaded about this. You made no secret of how you felt about fathering a child. There's no need to pretend you've had a miraculous change of heart. Not when you're only doing it out of some misguided sense of duty.

"I accepted enough charity to last a lifetime long before my eighteenth birthday, and I'm not about to be a burden to you or anyone else ever again. Not under any circumstances. I can take care of myself and my baby just fine, thank you."

"That's not why I'm here," he protested.

"Oh, no?" She eyed him with obvious disbelief.

"I'm not the coldhearted, calculating son of a bitch you seem to think I am. Granted, some of the things I've said and done have been contemptible. For that, I'm sorry...truly sorry. But I want what's best for you and the baby, and I'm willing to do whatever is necessary to see that you get it."

"You haven't heard a word I've said, have you? I don't *want* or *need* any—"

"Come back to Seattle with me, Jane, and let me look after you," Max cut in, taking her by the shoulders and turning her to face him. "Let me buy you an apartment, or better yet, a house. A house with a yard. A child needs a yard to play in. I'll arrange for a housekeeper, a gardener, a chauffeur...whatever staff you need. And I'll provide the best prenatal care money can buy.''

"Stop, Max. Just...stop," she cried. Pulling free, she stood and backed away from him. "I am *not* going back to Seattle with you. And I'm certainly *not* letting you look after me. I'm perfectly content here in Serenity, and here is where I intend to stay."

As she turned and moved toward the door, Max stood, too. Going after her, he put his hands on her shoulders again, halting her flight.

"Even though it might not be best for you or the baby?" he asked. "What if there are complications? You can't tell me a hospital in a small town like Serenity can offer the same quality of care a hospital in a major city can."

Jane seemed to waver for a moment, then shrugged him off.

"Go home, Max. File for divorce and forget about me. Forget about *us*. Believe me, you'll be a lot happier and so will I."

Before he could stop her again, she opened the screen door and slipped into the house. A few seconds later, the inner door swung shut with a finality he couldn't refute.

Cursing under his breath, Max pounded his fist on the porch railing in frustration. The little clay pots of herbs jumped in unison, but he wasn't amused.

Damn, he had really dug himself into a hole this time, and getting out wasn't going to be anywhere near as easy as he had hoped. He'd hurt Jane even more deeply than he had thought. Repairing the damage he'd done was going to take time, as well as effort. But that was the only way he'd have a chance of winning her back.

Winning her back...?

Was that really what he'd still had in mind? he wondered, taken aback. As he headed down the porch steps, he admitted, albeit reluctantly, that it most certainly was.

He had told himself he was only looking out for her well-being, but now he realized that he'd been motivated by a much stronger emotion than simple concern. He wanted his wife back—his wife *and* his child. And he was going to do whatever it took to get them back.

The desperate fear of losing them as he'd lost Alyssa and *their* child would probably never stop haunting him. But that didn't mean he had to let it rule his life any longer. He had missed out on so much already because he'd been afraid to love again. Now he'd been given a second chance at happiness, one he had come much too close to destroying.

Making amends to Jane was going to be difficult, but not impossible. Sooner or later, with patience and persistence, he would whittle away at her defenses, and he would gain her trust again. He had to. The alternative was too bleak to be considered.

She had won the first round, but he wasn't down for the count yet. He wasn't going to let her run him off no matter how hard she tried. Or how much he deserved it. He had made a lot of mistakes where she was concerned. He had asked her to trust him, then turned around and betrayed that trust—not once, but twice. He knew he had no right to expect her to give him another chance. But he was determined to prove that he was worthy of one.

His terror at the prospect of losing her in the throes of childbirth had been the catalyst that had sent him fleeing into the night. He had thought that if he could distance himself from her physically, he could also distance himself from her emotionally.

But it had already been too late for that. She had come to mean too much to him. Now that he could finally admit it to himself, he had to find a way to convince her of it, too.

Unfortunately, the one thing he couldn't do was offer an honest explanation of why he'd behaved so abominably last night. As he had acknowledged earlier, telling Jane about Alyssa's death was definitely out of the question. He would have to find another way to regain her regard.

Just staying in Serenity seemed the most likely way to accomplish that. His presence would surely count for something. He'd certainly have lots of opportunities to get her attention. And once he had that, anything would be possible.

Max returned to the bed-and-breakfast without further delay, walking swiftly down the sidewalk despite the rising heat. In his room, he dialed the number of the apartment and prepared to eat a full serving of crow.

He understood now what Calvin had been trying to tell him. Why the butler hadn't come right out and said that Jane was pregnant wasn't much of puzzle, either. Jane had probably sworn him to silence. And with good reason, Max reminded himself, recalling how he had reacted when her secret had finally been revealed.

As concisely as he could, Max explained the situation to Calvin. To his surprise, the butler responded with a measure of apology, as well as sympathy.

"I wish I could have told you, but a promise is a promise," he said.

"You tried to warn me as best you could under the circumstances," Max assured him. "Seems I am a total moron, after all."

"Not necessarily, Max. You're still in Serenity, aren't you? I also sense a change of heart on your part, and a willingness to make amends. So I wouldn't say all is lost just yet."

"I certainly hope not."

"What is the plan?"

"I'm flying home tonight, but only so I can make arrangements to come back here and stay indefinitely. Convincing Jane that I'm not the son of a bitch I seemed to be last night is going to take some time, and I can't do that from Seattle."

"Tell me what I can do to help, and I'll get right on it."

Max did just that, then called the airline, and finally spoke to the proprietors of the bed-and-breakfast. He was going to need a base of operations, and their property would suit his purposes just fine. By midafternoon, he was on his way back to San Antonio.

He was reluctant to be away even a few days, but he had responsibilities in Seattle he couldn't ignore completely. Too many people depended on him for their livelihood. But once he had made the arrangements necessary to guarantee Hamilton Enterprises would run smoothly during his extended absence, he would be back. Fortunately, many of the checks and balances were already firmly in place. Activating them should take less than a week.

Then he could concentrate on his wife and child. They meant more to him than anything else, and he intended to do his damnedest to become a permanent part of their lives.

Chapter Fourteen

"**H**e's here again," Emma announced, her voice
tinged with amusement, as well as exasperation.
"Right on schedule."

"So?" Jane glanced up from the flower bed she had
been weeding and shrugged carelessly.

"So maybe you ought to at least talk to him
or...something. It's been six weeks since he first came
to Serenity, and I get the feeling he's planning on being around for a while. He seems awfully determined
to see you again, too. He's come calling at least ten
times since he's been here."

Jane's only reply was an unladylike snort.

"Look, he's obviously not going to give up and go
away. And if the look on his face is any indication,
he's more than ready to grovel at your feet. Honestly,
Jane, I'm beginning to feel just a twinge of sympathy

for the guy. Why don't you at least see what he has to say for himself?''

"What I should do is call the police and report that I'm being stalked by a...by a..."

"A man willing to do penance for his sins?" Emma suggested. "Come on, Jane, he's not hanging around Serenity just waiting to do something dastardly. I honestly and truthfully believe he wants nothing more than to apologize for acting like a jerk. All you have to do is give him the chance.''

"He's gotten to you, hasn't he?"

Lumbering to her feet gracelessly, Jane dusted her hands on the seat of her bright red shorts, then straightened the hem of her sleeveless, red-and-white-polka-dot T-shirt. Even though it was almost the end of September, the heat of what had begun to seem like an endless summer still lingered in Serenity.

"Not exactly," Emma hedged.

"Hah!" Jane eyed her friend narrowly. "Rumor has it *that man* living at the Bergers' bed-and-breakfast comes to the library occasionally and has long talks with you. But only when I'm not there, I might add.''

"Maybe a couple of times lately," Emma admitted. Then, a twinkle in her green eyes, she continued. "But there's no need to be jealous. All he wants to talk about is you.''

"I'm *not* jealous. However, I am highly displeased. Whose side are you on, anyway?" Jane demanded, only half teasing.

"Yours, of course." Emma gave her a reassuring hug. "However, I really think you ought to give Max another chance. He knows he treated you badly, and he seems truly sorry. He's also concerned about you...both of you," she added, patting Jane's tummy.

"Only out of a sense of duty," Jane insisted.

"I think there's more to it than that. He's rented all the rooms at the Bergers', and from what Trudi Berger told me, he's set up some sort of command center so he can run his business from there. Why go to all that trouble just to ease his conscience? He could do that by having his accountant mail you a check once a month."

Jane had to admit that most of what Emma had said was true. Max had taken up residence in Serenity almost six weeks ago, and since then, he had waged a quiet campaign to return to her good graces. He hadn't foisted himself on her in any crude or obnoxious ways. And he hadn't staged any accidental meetings around town, either.

Jane had seen him at a distance several times, always unexpectedly, but considering the size of Serenity, that wasn't unusual. He hadn't seemed aware of her, though. And she certainly hadn't gone out of her way to call attention to herself.

What Max *had* done was call at Emma's house on Wednesday evenings and Sunday afternoons, regular as clockwork. So far, Jane had refused to see him. But much to her dismay, her resistance to his overtures was beginning to wear down.

Her curiosity about what, exactly, he wanted of her had been growing steadily as the weeks went by. She had most assuredly made her feelings clear at their last meeting. She wasn't going back to Seattle with him, and she wasn't accepting any financial help, either. She had returned the check he'd sent via her lawyer, and would do the same with any others that arrived in Emma's mailbox.

As for rekindling any kind of relationship with

him—platonic or otherwise—she would really rather not. She had talked tough six weeks ago, but she wasn't as immune to his masculine charms as she would have liked to be.

All too often lately, Jane had awakened in the midst of a sexually stimulating dream so vivid she had rolled over in her bed, still half-asleep, and reached for Max. Each time, she had been disgusted with herself. Not only for dreaming about him, but also for being disappointed at finding herself alone.

She couldn't deny that Max still had some claim to her heart. But that didn't mean she had to do anything about it. As long as she stayed as far away from him as possible, she wouldn't be tempted to say or do anything she would regret.

Giving in to him, even in a small way, would only encourage him to come around more often. Eventually, she imagined he would wear her down completely. Then, when he came to the inevitable conclusion that fatherhood really wasn't up his alley, after all, he would abandon her yet again, leaving her to cope with a deeper, more abiding anguish than she'd ever experienced before.

Jane simply could not believe that a man would insist on a childless marriage unless he was dead set against parenting. And Max's behavior had done nothing to disprove her theory. He had insisted that she didn't understand his ill-considered actions, but he hadn't given her an alternative explanation.

He had talked about responsibility, instead, and that just wasn't good enough for her. She knew firsthand the kind of life a child had when he or she was looked upon as a burden to bear. Her child was never going to endure that particular brand of unhappiness. Not as long as she had breath in her body. And should something happen to her, Emma would step in. Her friend had already agreed to be the little one's godmother, and Jane trusted her implicitly.

"So, made up your mind yet?" Emma prodded, interrupting her reverie. "Shall I dash his hopes again and send him away, or invite him in for a glass of tea while you take a shower and change into something pretty?"

Jane knew she should tell Emma to send Max away, but maybe she could get her point across more forcefully by speaking to him herself. So far, ignoring him hadn't really helped her cause, and she really hated to see him waste his time on something so futile.

"All right, invite him in," she said at last, starting toward the back door. "I'll be down in a few minutes."

She would shower, but only because she couldn't stand feeling so hot and gritty. And she would put on her yellow sundress, but only because it was one of the coolest, most comfortable items of clothing in her maternity wardrobe. Then she would talk to Max—briefly. And hopefully, that would be the end of that.

Twenty minutes later, feeling somewhat refreshed, Jane breezed into the kitchen, confident that she could turn this encounter with Max into her last.

She caught sight of him several seconds before he realized she was there. Halting by the counter, she gazed at him with a longing that rose unbidden. He sat at the table, his back half-turned to her, his bare legs—stretched out in front of him—casually crossed at the ankles.

He wore a plain white T-shirt that hugged his broad shoulders, tailored navy blue shorts and an old pair of deck shoes. Surprisingly, he had allowed his dark hair to grow shaggy. Wisps of it curled invitingly against the back of his neck. He'd also acquired a tan over the past few weeks that had turned his skin a delectable shade of bronze.

Almost all trace of the austere businessman she had married seemed to have disappeared. In his place was someone Jane found herself wanting to know in spite of everything. A man who had set aside the running of his company to be near her. A man who now seemed oddly vulnerable.

A man who glanced up from the Sunday paper he'd been thumbing through to see her standing there, then rose slowly, gazing at her with gray eyes so warm and hungry that her heart missed a beat.

Get a grip, she warned herself, her hand going automatically to her now burgeoning belly. Against her palm, the baby moved as it always seemed to do whenever Max was near.

Hi, Daddy. Look at me. See how much I've grown.

To Jane's surprise, Max did just that, the hunger in his eyes turning to wonder as his gaze drifted down her body, stopping at the very place where her hand rested. He started toward her, then stopped, looking up apologetically, as if he had forgotten himself.

"Hello, Jane."

"Hello, Max."

Nervously, she glanced around, looking for Emma, but her friend wasn't there. However, on the table sat a plate of chicken sandwiches along with a bowl of sliced peaches and a pitcher of cream.

Traitor, Jane thought, but without any real rancor. Considering how her stomach was growling, she was too grateful for the lunch her friend had so thoughtfully prepared to be angry or upset.

"You look...lovely," Max said.

"Thank you."

Blushing, she took a glass from the cabinet, then crossed to the refrigerator. She knew he was exaggerating. She'd scraped her wet hair into a twist at the nape of her neck, and hadn't bothered to add even a slight touch of makeup to her face. But his compliment pleased her anyway.

"Where's Emma?" she asked, breaking the silence that suddenly stretched between them as she filled her glass with milk.

"She said something about taking a basket of tomatoes to a friend of hers—Margaret Griffin," he replied.

"Oh." Glass in hand, Jane turned to join Max at the table.

"She thought you would be ready for lunch, and since I hadn't eaten yet..." Max's words trailed off as he held out a chair for her. "I hope you don't mind."

"No, of course not," she replied, gesturing toward the chair he had vacated.

Jane helped herself to a sandwich, then spooned peaches into one of the small dishes Emma had left on the table and added a dollop of cream. Wordlessly, Max followed suit.

They ate quietly for a few minutes. Glancing at her husband surreptitiously, Jane wished he would say something, anything, to give her a clue why he was there. But he seemed content to let her take the lead.

"Emma said you've been staying at the Bergers' bed-and-breakfast for the past few weeks. Any special reason for that?'' she asked at last, having taken the edge off her hunger.

Lately, her appetite had been ravenous, but Dr. Harrison had assured her that was normal. As long as she ate healthy, well-balanced meals, her baby would thrive. And at the same time, her weight gain should stay within the recommended limit.

''A very special reason, as a matter of fact,'' Max stated simply. ''You're here.''

''Oh, Max. I thought I made it clear how I feel—'' she began, unable to hide her exasperation.

''And I thought I made it clear how I feel,'' he cut in gently, his gaze unwavering.

''You did. You made it *very* clear that you *didn't* want children.''

''At one time, yes. But I wasn't thinking straight then. Now I am.'' He reached out and took her hand in his, tightening his grip when she tried to pull away. ''Our baby means as much to me as it does to you. Please, Jane, don't shut me out completely because of the mistakes I've made in the past.''

She stared at him without speaking as he lifted her hand to his lips and kissed her fingertips.

''All I'm asking is that you give me a chance to prove how much I care about the two of you,'' he added.

Unable to bear his scrutiny any longer, Jane looked away. She couldn't deny the anguish she'd seen in his eyes or doubt the sincerity she'd heard in his voice. But was his declaration enough to warrant putting her own heart on the line again?

Fool me once, shame on you. Fool me twice, shame on me.

Dare she set herself up for another fall? Or would the third time be the charm?

"I don't know, Max...." she said, weighed down by indecision.

If he was being honest with her and she turned him away, she would be forfeiting so very, very much—for herself, as well as for her child. But if he was playing some kind of macho mind game with her in an attempt to gain the upper hand, they would be better off on their own.

"I know you're leery of me, and I understand why. I've already let you down too many times. I also know that I have no right to ask you to trust me again. But I can't just walk away. I can't and I *won't.*"

Max's grave tone left no doubt in Jane's mind of how tenacious he intended to be, and trying to hold him at bay would take more energy than she could afford to expend.

Dr. Harrison had advised her to avoid putting herself under stress as much as possible—not only physically, but emotionally—for the duration of her pregnancy. Constantly having to face a barrage of inner turmoil could very likely cause all sorts of complications to arise.

Acquiescing to some of Max's wishes might actually be the wisest thing to do. Somewhat mollified, he wouldn't be quite so apt to put added pressure on her. At the same time, perhaps some of her uncertainty might ease, as well.

She didn't have to give herself over to him completely. She could, and most certainly *would,* hold a part of herself back until after the baby was born. Then she could consider her options with a clearer head.

Max would surely have ample opportunity to show

his true colors over the next three months. According to the books she'd been reading, the last stage of pregnancy could be a trying time for even the most loving couples.

He wouldn't be able to ignore her condition. The baby would be there between them every single day— either drawing them together or forcing them apart. As long as she didn't get her hopes up, the less-desirable outcome shouldn't affect her unduly.

"So, what exactly do you have in mind?" she asked, aware that he was still holding her hand, and that his thumb was now toying with the wedding ring she hadn't yet been able to discard.

"Any chance I can talk you into going back to Seattle?" he asked, one corner of his mouth quirking up.

"None at all," she stated flatly.

"Well, then, how about dinner Tuesday night after the childbirth class at the hospital?" he suggested without missing a beat.

"How do you know about that?" Jane couldn't hide her surprise as she met his gaze.

He looked back at her, smiling sheepishly.

"I asked around about stuff like that and took a wild guess. The timing seemed right. You *are* going, aren't you?"

"With Emma. I asked her to be my coach."

"I'd like to go, too."

He could have asked to take Emma's place, but he hadn't. He wanted only to be included. Jane couldn't see any reason to refuse him. He was her baby's father, after all.

"I can't see any problem with that."

"Good." His smile glowed with such warmth that Jane found herself smiling, too.

"As for dinner…"

"Emma's more than welcome to join us," Max hastened to assure her.

"I'll tell her."

"Then I guess I'll see you at the hospital Tuesday evening."

He stood and tucked his hands in his pockets.

Feeling slightly off balance, Jane stood, too. He really wasn't pushing his luck, she thought. He hadn't offered to provide their transportation, and now he was leaving of his own volition.

"The class starts at five-thirty," she said, for want of anything better.

"I know. I'll be there." He turned and headed for the short hallway that led to the living room. "Thanks for the lunch."

"You're welcome," she replied, trailing after him.

At the front door, Max faced her again.

"Tuesday, then," he repeated, reaching out and touching her cheek.

"Yes, Tuesday," she murmured, savoring the gentleness of his caress.

Had she been a cat, she would have rubbed against him, purring with delight.

"You *are* lovely." Smiling, he lowered his hand to her tummy and curved his long, lithe fingers around her reverently. "Both of you."

A moment later, he slipped out the door and was gone.

Jane stood in the doorway long afterward, gazing into the sunlit distance, her own hand where his had been as a silly smile tugged at the corners of her mouth.

No doubt about it. She had Pushover stamped on her forehead. But just then, she didn't really care. With surprising suddenness, anything seemed possible again. Even happily-ever-after.

Chapter Fifteen

"Are you sure you don't want to join us for dinner? I made reservations at the Veranda," Max said.

"Thanks for the invitation, but I have some paperwork to catch up on," Emma replied, offering him a sly smile. "But you two go ahead."

"You really are welcome to come with us," Jane insisted as the three of them left the hospital and headed toward the parking lot.

"I know, but I'll have to take a rain check."

"You said that last Tuesday," Jane reminded her.

"Believe me, I would *never* miss dinner at the Veranda without good reason."

Listening to their byplay as he walked along with them, Max felt his smile widen into a grin. He really enjoyed their company. So much so that the Tuesday-night childbirth classes at Serenity General Hospital had become the highlight of his week. But even more, he had enjoyed having Jane all to himself afterward as he had last Tuesday night, and it seemed, as he would again tonight—thanks to Emma's deft maneuvering.

Gradually over the past three weeks, she had become an ally in his quest to win back Jane's love. She had stuck to Jane like glue that first Tuesday night. Since then, however, she had been easing herself out of the picture, making it possible for him to spend more and more time alone with his wife. And she had done so with such skill, Jane hadn't seemed to notice.

Either that, or his wife hadn't really minded being on her own with him. Max hoped that was the case, but he couldn't really be sure. And because he couldn't, he had been hesitant to push his luck.

Seeing Jane on Tuesday nights and again on Sunday afternoons—thanks again to Emma and her invitations to Sunday dinner—hadn't been nearly enough to satisfy his longings. But he had taken what he could get, and tried to be grateful.

He had miles of fences to mend before he could expect anything more from his wife. Granted, she no longer seemed quite so wary around him. Still, he knew that one false move on his part could all too easily lay waste to the ground he had gained lately.

Slowly, he continually reminded himself. Take it slowly, and she'll trust you again one day.

Outside, the night air was refreshingly brisk and bracing. Mid-October in Serenity had been a welcome delight after the lingering heat and humidity of summer. With the onset of what the locals called blue northers, the days had begun to dawn crisp and clear, and the evenings were now scented with the wood smoke that drifted lazily from chimneys all over town.

Jane shivered delicately as they walked across the lot, clasping her arms over her chest. Instinctively, Max put an arm around her shoulders and drew her closer to his side. She hesitated a moment, then leaned into his embrace.

"I didn't think I'd need a jacket," she murmured apologetically.

She wore slim black knit pants that showcased her long, lovely legs and a hunter green turtleneck sweater that still hung loosely over her belly.

"You don't," Max growled teasingly, his mouth pressed to her ear. "You've got me to keep you warm."

She glanced up at him, a startled look in her eyes, then smiled shyly as she lowered her gaze again.

"I guess I do, don't I?" she agreed. "And a good thing, too, since I have a feeling my jacket probably doesn't fit anymore."

"I'd offer to let you borrow one of mine, but then I wouldn't have an excuse to put my arm around you."

"Not necessarily."

"In that case, you can come back to the Bergers' with me after dinner and choose whichever one you want," he said, emboldened by her bantering.

"I might just do that."

"All right, you two. Enough cuddling in public," Emma warned in a teasing tone. "This is a small town. People will talk."

"I think people are already talking," Max retorted ruefully.

"They are?" Jane asked, obviously surprised. "About us? Why?"

"Well, it's no secret that the two of you are married, and you have to admit your living arrangements are rather...odd," Emma said.

"Oh, well, yes..." Jane agreed. Then, with a defiant tip of her chin, she added, "Lucky for them, too. Otherwise, they'd have to find someone else to gossip about, wouldn't they?"

"So we're doing them a public service?" Max quipped, unaccountably pleased by her attitude.

He would have had a much easier time of it had she been the type to be swayed by public opinion. But he wouldn't have admired her nearly as much as he did at that moment.

"We most certainly are," she affirmed with a nod of her head as they halted beside the car he'd leased upon his return from Seattle.

"See you later, Jane," Emma called out as she crossed to her own car and unlocked the door. "Good night, Max."

"Good night, Emma."

"I won't be too late," Jane promised.

"Better not. I've got pages of new titles for you to input into our computer system tomorrow, and I don't want you falling asleep on me...again."

"That's only happened once or twice. Maybe three times at the most," Jane argued.

"Actually, I recall *four* occasions. But, hey, who's counting?"

With a wave of her hand, Emma slipped into her car, then started the engine and pulled out of the lot.

"Maybe you should cut back on the number of hours you've been putting in," Max suggested—not without some hesitation—as he helped Jane into his car. "For the baby's sake."

He knew she didn't like to be fussed over, so he tried hard to keep his worry to himself. He didn't want to transmit even a hint of the fear for her he battled on a daily basis. But he couldn't keep from reminding her that she didn't have to work at the library. There were other, less taxing ways she could keep busy during the last stage of her pregnancy while he saw to her financial needs.

Of course, he knew better than to say as much to her outright. However, he had found that mentioning the baby's welfare was often all it took to convince her to set aside her pride.

"Actually, I've been thinking about doing that," she admitted as he started the car. "But I feel like I should be doing *something*. Just sitting around Emma's house, twiddling my thumbs, would drive me crazy."

"You could give me a hand analyzing the data coming in on the HED laptop promotion Doug Jacoby initiated," Max said, putting into words the plan he'd been formulating over the past few days. "The numbers aren't as high as we anticipated, and for the life of me, I can't seem to figure out why. I can't find any fault with Jacoby's concept and application, but I keep getting the feeling that I'm missing something obvious.

"Since you weren't directly involved in the project, maybe you would be able to recognize the glitch. I'd put you on the payroll as a consultant, of course, and I guarantee you can take all the naps you want without any hassle from me."

Jane's eyes lit up as she glanced at him, yet she didn't leap at his offer.

"Sounds like an interesting problem to solve," she said. "But are you sure you really need my help?"

"I wouldn't have asked you otherwise," he assured her truthfully, aware that she would have known immediately if he'd merely made work for her. "Not with the consulting fee I'm going to have to pay you."

"Per diem, of course, at the going rate."

"Yes."

Looking over at her, Max saw a smile playing at the corners of her mouth.

"I'll have to talk to Emma. I don't want to leave her in the lurch."

"Just let me know what you decide."

"I will."

As he pulled into the parking lot of the Veranda, Max could barely hide *his* grin. Another barrier between them seemed to be on the verge of collapse. They had always worked well together in the past. He had every faith they would do so again, and in the process draw even closer.

The restaurant, decorated in an old-fashioned Victorian motif, complete with gas lamps flickering in wall sconces, wasn't too crowded that evening. Having already proved to be a better than average patron, Max was offered a table in a quiet corner. He gratefully accepted, holding Jane's chair for her, then seating himself beside her. He ordered a glass of red wine for himself and, at Jane's request, a glass of ginger ale for her.

As he watched in amusement, Jane pored over the menu the waitress had handed her, debating aloud the merits of grilled fish over a pasta dish smothered in rich cream sauce. She finally decided on the fish, admitting that it would be healthier. Aware that she really craved the pasta dish, Max chose it, then suggested they share. She agreed quite readily as she helped herself to a hot roll from the basket the waitress brought with their drinks.

The first Tuesday he had suggested they have dinner together after the childbirth class, Emma had joined them, and the conversation had been fairly impersonal. Last Tuesday, he and Jane had been on their own, but she had still been wary enough of him that he'd been forced to mind his manners. Tonight, however, she seemed much more at ease.

She had been surprisingly receptive to his tentatively offered overtures. Granted, she hadn't made any promises—either to go back to the Bergers' bed-and-breakfast with him or to help with the HED data analysis—but she hadn't turned him down flat. As far as he was concerned, they were definitely making progress. Now all he had to do was maintain a positive frame of mind.

Which certainly wouldn't be hard for him to do tonight. Just being with Jane lightened his heart. Always had, he realized, and always would.

Looking back, he couldn't believe he had once thought he would be satisfied with her companionship alone. He wanted to share everything with her that life had to offer, especially raising a family, and God willing, he would have that opportunity.

"What do you think about the childbirth classes?" Max asked after the waitress served their salads.

"Very interesting," Jane replied. "I don't have anything to compare with, of course. But I think I've chosen the best method for me. I wasn't sure I had the stamina for Lamaze. All that panting..." She offered him a wry smile. "When I was reading up on alternate schools of thought, the Bradley method really appealed. I like the idea of slow, deep breathing while focusing inward and working with my body. How about you? Any thoughts on the subject?"

"I like what I've heard so far. But then, our instructor did say Bradley was the first to promote the husband-as-coach method of labor and delivery." He returned her smile, adding, "I know you've asked Emma to be with you when the time comes, but I'd like to be there, too."

"I can't see any problem with that," she said.

Until then, Max hadn't been sure how Jane would feel about having him present during the birth of their baby. Knowing that he would be welcome gratified him deeply. But fear also gnawed at his heart. Refusing to let it drag him down, he beat it back as best he could.

They finished their salads in companionable silence, then sat back as the waitress cleared their plates and served their entrées. As she walked away, Jane picked up her fork, paused, then looked over at him.

"I promise I'll save half the pasta for you," he said, his voice laced with amusement. "And I won't even insist that you share your fish. You *are* eating for two."

"I'll share," she replied. "But that wasn't what I had on my mind."

"What, then?"

"Actually, I was wondering...are you going to be busy Friday morning?"

"Not especially."

"Well, I'm scheduled for another sonogram at ten o'clock. I thought maybe you might like to come along and have your first look at the baby."

Max couldn't have asked for a more precious gift. His heart brimmed with joy, and oddly, his eyes stung with tears. He blinked hard, willing them away as he nodded gravely.

"Yes, I would like that very much." Holding her gaze, he reached out and touched her cheek. "Thank you for asking me."

"You're welcome."

Obviously embarrassed, Jane turned her attention to her meal, and Max did likewise, heartened beyond imagining. Again, they ate in companionable silence. After a few minutes of quiet contemplation, however, Max decided to tender an invitation of his own.

"I've been wanting to drive down to San Antonio for the past couple of weeks, but the weather's been so hot. Now that it's finally cooled off a bit, I thought I might go on Saturday. Why don't you come along? We can do a little shopping for the baby."

When Jane didn't answer immediately, he feared he had overstepped the invisible boundaries she had set. She toyed with the carrots on her plate, a thoughtful expression on her face, then finally met his gaze.

"Just for the day?" she asked.

"Unless you'd like to stay longer," he replied, trying not to sound too eager.

"Not this time."

"Then we can drive back Saturday evening."

"There are a few things I need that I haven't been able to find here." Adroitly she exchanged a piece of her fish for a portion of his pasta, then glanced at him again. "All right, I'll go with you," she agreed. "What time do you want to leave?"

"Whatever time is good for you."

"How about eight-thirty? I know a little place in Bandera where we can stop for breakfast. Then we can have lunch in San Antonio. There's a wonderful Mexican restaurant—actually a restaurant and bakery—at the market.'' She paused, a blush tingeing her cheeks. ''I'm not really *that* fixated on food,'' she insisted.

''Does that mean you don't want to finish the last of my pasta?''

''Well...''

They both laughed. Then, as their gazes met, and they sobered slightly, Max sensed a new tenderness developing between them.

''How about dessert?''

''Mmm, better not tonight.''

While Max indulged in a glass of brandy and a frothy cup of cappuccino, Jane opted for herbal tea laced with a dollop of honey. They discussed their trip to San Antonio a little more, then Max paid their bill and they walked out to the car. As she had earlier, Jane shivered in the cool night air.

''The offer of a jacket still stands,'' Max said, slipping his arm around her.

''Thanks, but I think I'll look for something in San Antonio. Maybe a wool cape or a fleecy shawl.''

Much as Max wanted a little time alone with her, *all* alone in a private place, he knew better than to insist.

''Sounds like a good idea,'' he agreed, albeit regretfully.

The drive to Emma's house took only a few minutes. There, Max walked Jane to the front door, the soft glow of the porch light guiding their steps. A lamp shone in the living room window, and another light had been lit in one of the upstairs bedrooms, as well, signaling the probability that her friend was still awake.

''I'll see you on Friday at ten o'clock,'' he said. ''At Dr. Harrison's office, right?''

"Yes, at Dr. Harrison's office," she replied.

"I'll be looking forward to it."

"Me, too."

Max hadn't intended to kiss her, but the way she gazed at him, her eyes glimmering with warmth, he simply couldn't help himself. He reached for her and gently drew her close, bent his head and brushed his lips over hers, giving her every opportunity to push him away.

Instead, she moved closer to him, put her arms around his neck and kissed him back. Really kissed him, her lips roving over his with a hunger that startled him. Luckily, he managed to keep his wits about him. Yet he couldn't stop himself completely from deepening their contact. He delved into her mouth, sliding his tongue over hers, savoring the taste of mint tea that lingered on her breath.

Then he raised his head, planted a chaste kiss on her forehead and resolutely turned away.

"See you on Friday," he said, smiling as he glanced back at her.

"Yes, Friday," she answered, a wondrously starry look in her eyes.

Tempted as he was to go back to her, he didn't. But another night, he would—another night very soon. He knew it in his heart.

Chapter Sixteen

Jane sat in the passenger's seat of Max's car and gazed contentedly at the passing scenery as they drove along the winding, hilly country road. Autumn had finally begun to touch the trees with shades of yellow, red and gold, brightening the landscape, and the sun shone in a clear blue sky, promising pleasant weather.

They had stopped for breakfast as planned in the small town of Bandera, so her hunger had been temporarily assuaged. Then they had talked for a while in a desultory manner, agreeing on an itinerary of sorts for the day ahead. With a limited amount of time to spend, they had wanted to be sure they covered as much ground as possible.

Shopping first, they had decided, at one of the large malls on the outskirts of the city. Then a late lunch followed by some sight-seeing. And dinner, of course,

Max had teasingly insisted, to fortify them for the drive back to Serenity.

Their conversation had dwindled after that, and with Jane's permission, Max had slipped a CD into the car's stereo system. As the soothing strains of a violin concerto had filled the air, Jane's thoughts had drifted back to the previous day. And she found herself trying—yet again—to sort out her feelings for her husband.

Just when she thought she knew him, he would say or do something that forced her to reassess. Her thoughts and emotions seemed to be in constant turmoil, and lately, she had begun to feel as if she were on one of those whirly-twirly carnival rides spinning wildly out of control.

Almost ten weeks ago, Jane had been sure Max's reappearance at Emma's house had been prompted by nothing more than a sense of duty. She had also been sure that eventually he would give up and go away. Running Hamilton Enterprises at such a distance had to be hard. And, as Emma had pointed out, he could have alleviated any guilt he suffered by sending her a check on a regular basis.

Instead, he had stayed on week after week until she had finally relented. Spending time in his company, she had seen another side to him. One that had appealed to her so much she hadn't been able to stop herself from kissing him in a most disconcerting manner.

But she had yet to let down her guard completely. One kiss, no matter how sensually satisfying, wasn't nearly enough to convince her to throw caution to the wind. Memories of his past behavior were still too fresh in her mind.

Yesterday, however, Max had come closer to re-
deeming himself than ever. Watching his reaction as
he saw their baby's image on the ultrasound monitor,
Jane had been sorely tempted to believe that becoming
a father really did mean as much to him as he kept
quietly insisting it did.

He had sat by her side during the sonogram, holding
on to her hand, his eyes glued to the screen as Dr.
Harrison moved the transducer over her abdomen. The
nurse had been able to point out the baby's head, the
curve of its spine, a tiny arm and a leg tucked up to
its tummy. Only the baby's sex hadn't been obvious,
but Jane hadn't minded. She liked the idea of being
surprised in the delivery room.

As for Max, the look of sheer wonder on his face
was one Jane wouldn't soon forget. And the awe she
had heard in his voice still rang in her ears.

Look, Jane. Can you believe it? Our child...so tiny,
yet so...perfect....

How many men would respond to their first look at
a baby they didn't want with such unabashed rapture?
Surely only an actor of the highest caliber could fake
the kind of emotion Max had expressed in Dr. Harrison's office. And what reason would he have for pretending? He certainly had nothing to gain by it. At
least not that she could see.

Which only made his initial demand for a childless
marriage that much harder for her to fathom. Unless
she was sadly mistaken, the child she carried in her
womb had already staked a claim on Max's heart. But
how could that have happened when so much of what
he'd said and done in the past seemed to negate such
a possibility?

Max had been brutally frank about his feelings

when he'd proposed to her ten months ago. What had prompted that? More important, what had caused his sudden change of heart? And how permanent would it prove to be?

Jane wished she had the courage to ask, but she wasn't sure she was ready to hear whatever answer he chose to give.

"The exit for the 410 Loop is just ahead. Do we want to head north or south?" Max asked, drawing her back to the present moment.

Looking around, Jane realized they were on the interstate highway just outside the San Antonio city limits. She had been so lost in thought, she hadn't even noticed when they had left the two-lane road.

"North," she replied. "Then we'll take the third exit. I can't remember the street name, but there will be a sign advertising the mall about a mile or so before we come to it."

Max negotiated the Saturday-morning traffic with ease. Within a few minutes, they were parked on the lot and on their way into the larger of the two department stores that anchored each end of the shopping complex.

"Why don't we agree on a time and meet back here then?" Jane asked, glancing at her watch. "That way, we can get our shopping done much faster."

"Actually, I don't have any shopping to do for myself, so we might as well stay together. I promise I won't look bored, sigh or roll my eyes. And I'll carry all your packages without complaint," he replied with a boyish grin.

"Well, if you're sure you don't mind tagging along..." Jane demurred.

"Not at all. Where to first?"

"The coat department," she stated without further hesitation.

Jane found a lovely black cashmere cape that had been cut full enough to see her through the last months of her pregnancy, yet had been tailored in such a way that she would be able to use it afterward, as well.

Next, she headed for the maternity department, where she went on a real buying spree. She splurged on another turtleneck sweater in a bright shade of red, a long-sleeved red-and-white-striped shirt to use with the denim jumper she wore that day, a pair of softly faded, supercomfy jeans and a simple but elegant black wool dress to see her through the holiday season.

Smiling apologetically, she piled her purchases into Max's arms, then headed for the ladies' room while he took them out to the car. Upon his return, they decided to take a walk through the mall itself.

At the far end, they came upon a store specializing in baby clothes and furniture. Max's eyes lit up immediately. Grabbing her by the hand, he led her through the doorway, then urged her to choose whatever she wanted to outfit the spare room at Emma's as a nursery—at his expense.

Jane couldn't help but protest. The store featured only top-of-the-line merchandise, and her feelings about taking charity hadn't changed. But Max insisted in such a heartfelt tone that she found it impossible to resist further. He obviously wasn't offering out of a sense of obligation. And she couldn't—in good conscience—deny him the pleasure of providing for his child.

At the very least, she needed a bed for the baby, and a changing table would be nice. Perhaps a mechanical swing, and yes, a chest to match the bed. Max insisted she choose the necessary bedding and several outfits suitable for a boy or a girl, as well. And he blithely added a car seat, a stroller and a cuddly stuffed bear with an expression so enchanting Jane laughed out loud.

As the clerk tallied their purchases, Jane ran her hand over the bear's plush fur, overwhelmed by an emotion she was afraid to name.

"You look like you're about to cry," Max murmured, tucking a finger under her chin and lifting her face so that she couldn't avoid his probing gaze.

Hastily, she blinked back the tears that were, indeed, threatening to fall.

"You're being much too generous," she said, waving a hand at all the items stacked around the register, most of which would be delivered to Emma's within the next week or so.

"I just wanted to be sure our baby had everything he or she might need," he stated simply.

"But you didn't have to...."

"I know. I *wanted* to, Jane. You won't let me buy anything for you," he said, reminding her of the argument they'd had earlier when she'd been shopping for herself. "At least let me buy a few things for the baby."

"All right," she acquiesced, suddenly sorry that she had brought the subject up again.

She hadn't meant to spoil Max's joy in providing for their child. Actually, some small, secret part of her had gloried in it. The part of her that still insisted on hoping against hope.

"Here, you better look after Mr. Bear," Max said, as if sensing her sudden need to hold on to something.

"He looks like the type to get into big trouble if left unsupervised."

"He does, doesn't he?" she agreed, hugging the fuzzy creature to her chest. "What shall we call him? Just Mr. Bear?"

"He really should have a first name," Max said, gathering the bags containing the baby clothes and bedding, then taking Jane by the arm as they turned to leave the store. "Any ideas?"

"How about Bruiser?"

"Perfect." Max grinned as he met her gaze. "Bruiser Bear it is. Now, how about some lunch?"

"Mmm, I thought you'd never ask."

Jane gave Max directions to the Mexican market located in downtown San Antonio. They had lunch at Mi Tierra Bakery as she had suggested, indulging in steaming platters of enchiladas, rice and refried beans.

Afterward, they drove into the city center so Max could see the Alamo. Then, as the afternoon began to wane, they made their way to San Antonio's famous River Walk, where they strolled hand in hand, enjoying the crowds and the scenery.

"Having fun?" Max asked as they paused to watch a water taxi pass.

"Yes," Jane assured him. "Thanks for inviting me."

"You really know your way around."

"Only because of Emma. We used to come here occasionally when I first lived in Serenity, but the city's changed a lot since then. After I moved back, Emma suggested we ride over for old times' sake, and she gave me the grand tour."

"She's been a good friend to you, hasn't she?"

"A very good friend."

"I'm surprised she's never married."

"She was engaged to her high-school sweetheart, but he was killed in an automobile accident. It was really tragic. Her fiancé's brother was driving, but it wasn't his fault. She was devastated. She loved Teddy so much. I'm not sure she'll ever get over losing him."

"Maybe if the right man comes along..."

"Maybe," Jane agreed, though she wasn't thinking so much of Emma as of Max as she did.

Something about his tone and the way he'd squeezed her hand made her wonder if he was talking about himself, as well. Had he gotten over the loss of his first love? Was he now able to open his heart to her as she had once hoped he would?

How she wanted to believe that was possible. But her faith in him was still too shaky.

"When I talked to Calvin last night, he said to tell you hello," Max commented after a while.

They had crossed one of the narrow bridges spanning the river, and had begun to retrace their steps on the opposite side.

"Oh, really?" Jane queried with a smile. "He told me the same thing last night, too."

"He seemed pleased that we were seeing each other."

"Mmm..." Jane shrugged noncommittally. Then she added curiously, "Has he said anything to you about coming down just before the baby's due?"

"Several times. I get the feeling he doesn't exactly trust us with his godchild," Max said. "By the way, thanks for asking him. I have it on good authority the old curmudgeon was deeply honored."

"I couldn't think of anyone as trustworthy as he, and Emma, of course."

"I can't, either."

"I know they'll look after our baby if anything ever happens to us, and that's all that really matters to me."

"Only nothing is going to happen to us," Max stated succinctly. "We're going to grow old and gray watching our children grow up."

Jane wanted to agree with him, but she knew first-hand there were no guarantees in life. Her parents hadn't been that fortunate, and they had loved each other. How could she believe *she* would have better luck?

She and Max didn't have any foundation to fall back on. Their marriage had been built on shaky ground that had crumbled all too quickly. And rebuilding still remained—at least in her mind—a dubious proposition.

"That would be nice," she murmured by way of compromise.

"Very nice." Max squeezed her hand again, then released her so that he could slide his arm around her shoulders and draw her closer to his side.

She went willing enough, warmed by the gesture. Yet somewhere in the back of her mind, she thought—with the merest hint of cynicism—that most dreams *were* nice. Unfortunately, more often than not, real life turned out to be something else altogether.

By the time they had made a full circuit of the River Walk, the sun had dipped below the horizon. With the onset of evening, a festive atmosphere had taken over. Mariachi bands had begun to play in various restaurants, the music drifting out across the water. The number of people milling about, pausing to read posted menus or to eye the trinkets displayed in shop windows had also increased appreciably.

Max asked if she was ready for dinner, but surprisingly, Jane was more tired than hungry. Suddenly anxious to get home again, she suggested they head back to Serenity without further delay, and he easily agreed.

Much as Jane had enjoyed being with Max, she suddenly felt off balance. She desperately needed some time alone. Time to gather her wits about her before she did something foolish.

Throughout the day, Max had made no secret of the fact that he fully expected them to have a future together, and she had said nothing to dissuade him. Rather, she had let herself dream along with him.

Now she realized she was on the verge of getting more involved with him than might be wise, and that made her afraid. Not of Max, but of the power he was all too close to having over her again. The power to hurt her even more deeply than he'd already done.

Had he really changed so much? she asked herself yet again. Or was she only fooling herself?

She couldn't seem to come to a reasonable conclusion. Not when he looked at her with such longing. Not when he held her close and brushed his lips against her cheek. Not when he turned to face her, gathered her into his arms and held her, just held her with heartbreaking tenderness before he opened the car door for her.

As if sensing her need to withdraw, Max, too, retreated on the drive back to Serenity. He offered dinner again when they reached town, then accepted her refusal graciously. At Emma's, he unloaded her packages and carried them to the door. Following her directions, he stacked them just inside the entryway, then turned to leave.

"I guess I'll see you Tuesday night," he said.

"Actually…" she began, clutching Bruiser in her arms, then paused as he eyed her questioningly. She took a breath, mustered her courage and finally continued. "I thought maybe we could get together sooner. Say sometime tomorrow. Before or after Sunday dinner. To go over the HED data. That is, if the offer of a consulting job is still open."

She wasn't sure working with him was a good idea. But after today, she didn't think she could wait until Tuesday to see him again. She would probably be sorry, but it certainly wouldn't be the first time.

"It is," he assured her, a smile lighting his eyes. "And tomorrow would be fine."

"Come early, then. Around one o'clock. That will give us a couple of hours before we eat."

"I'll be here."

"Good night, then."

"Good night."

He closed the distance between them, put his hands on her shoulders and kissed her soundly on the mouth. Then, his smile widening, he ruffled the bear's furry head, turned and walked away.

Chapter Seventeen

With a muttered curse, Max eased off the gas pedal, allowing the car's speed to drop to the posted limit on the winding road leading to Serenity. He did not, under any circumstances, want to be stopped by an overzealous state trooper. Any further delay in getting back to town, and there was no telling what he would do.

The sense of trepidation that had been growing in him steadily since the night before now had him in a stranglehold that wouldn't ease until he knew that Jane was all right. And with his fear for her had come anger at himself, anger he might very well turn on anyone who tried to get in his way.

He should have never gone back to Seattle, not for any reason. But Jane and the baby had been fine when he left, he'd planned to be away only two nights and he had postponed the meeting with Hamilton Enterprises's East Coast distributor as long as he could.

Max hadn't factored in the possibility that his flight back to San Antonio would be canceled due to bad weather. And he certainly hadn't anticipated being unable to get in touch with Jane. Yesterday afternoon, last night and again early that morning when he'd finally arrived on the red-eye, he had called Emma's house. Each time he'd gotten her answering machine, and each time he had left a message for Jane to call Calvin. He had checked in with the butler one last time before he left the airport, but as of then, there had been no word from her.

Max had dozed on the plane out of sheer exhaustion, but his restless sleep had been plagued with nightmares. And since he'd been on the road, all sorts of worst-case scenarios had haunted his thoughts.

Had some unexpected complication arisen with Jane's pregnancy? Had she gone into labor prematurely? The baby wasn't due for another six weeks or so. Could it survive being born this early?

Max had every faith in Dr. Harrison and the quality of care provided at Serenity General Hospital. Of course, he'd had both the doctor and the hospital thoroughly investigated. But if the baby simply wasn't strong enough, even the best care in the world wouldn't do any good.

Or what if Jane herself had fallen ill? Worse, what if she had been injured in some way? Could she have gone out in the stormy weather they'd had yesterday and been involved in an automobile accident?

He couldn't think of any reason she would have had to leave the house under such conditions. They had talked Thursday night, but she hadn't mentioned any special plans for the day. And going off to work hadn't been a necessity, either.

With Emma's blessing, Jane had given up her job at the library almost a month ago. Since then, she had helped him with the HED data analysis, finding the glitch within a week, along with various other projects she'd been able to work on at her own pace.

His nerves frayed almost beyond bearing, Max finally reached Serenity. He drove straight to Emma's, pulled up at the curb outside her house with a screech of tires and hurried up the brick walkway.

He rang the bell insistently, then opened the unlatched screen door and banged on the brass knocker several times, as well. He was reaching for the door handle on the off chance that the inner door had also been left unlocked, when it swung open with a whoosh.

Caught off balance, he braced a hand on the door frame, then literally sagged against it with relief. Jane stood in the doorway, eyeing him quizzically, dressed in her slim-legged black pants and red turtleneck sweater, her hair pulled back in a sassy ponytail.

"Max...?" she began.

"Jeez, Janie, where have you been?" he demanded, cutting her off as he hauled her into his arms and hugged her fiercely, then ran a hand over her belly caressingly.

Against his palm, he felt the baby kick. They were all right—both of them. Sending up a silent prayer of thanks, he bent his head and pressed a kiss to his wife's forehead.

"Something came up unexpectedly yesterday morning." She slipped an arm around his waist and urged him into the house.

"You're okay, aren't you? You and the baby?" he asked, seeking her verbal reassurance as his gaze roved over her again.

"I'm just fine," she replied, leading him into the living room, then gesturing for him to sit on the sofa. "And the little one's been practicing gymnastics all morning, so I can safely say all's well there, too."

"So where have you and Emma been?"

Max sank onto the sofa gratefully, and slipped out of his jacket. Jane curled up beside him, tucking her legs up under her.

"Remember I told you about Emma's fiancé, Teddy?"

Max nodded.

"Well, Emma's grown quite close to his mother, Margaret, over the past few years. Margaret had gone to San Antonio for medical tests several days ago. She hadn't really thought there was anything seriously wrong, but early yesterday morning the doctors told her she would have to start chemotherapy first thing Monday morning.

"When Margaret called to relay the news, Emma insisted on going down to San Antonio so she could be with her over the weekend, as well as on Monday. Since Margaret already had her car there, and probably won't be able to drive for a while, I offered to give Emma a lift. That way, she'll be able to drive Margaret home when she's discharged from the hospital."

"You drove to San Antonio yesterday? In the midst of all the bad weather?"

Max eyed her incredulously, just the thought of what she'd done striking terror into his heart all over again.

"Actually, we missed most of it on the drive down,

and I waited until the worst was over before I headed back. Then I stopped for dinner along the way. That's why I didn't get in until late.''

''Too late to call Calvin?''

She looked away, obviously embarrassed.

''I was really tired. I didn't even think to check the answering machine for messages. I just went straight to bed.''

''What about when I called this morning? Where were you then?''

He didn't mean to sound as if he was giving her the third degree, but his panic had yet to recede completely. Not only knowing where she had been and what she had been doing, but also that she'd been safe all the while, went a long way toward banishing the more awful of his imaginings.

''Either in the shower or blow-drying my hair. I must have just missed hearing the telephone ring. When I finally remembered to check for messages, you were already on your way to Serenity. I called Calvin to put his mind at ease. But yesterday, before we left, I also called Trudi Berger and left a message for you. I assumed you'd go straight there when you got in last night.'' She rubbed his arm consolingly. ''I never realized you'd be so worried about me.''

''Trudi Berger...'' Max sighed and shook his head. ''Checking with her would have been the logical thing to do, wouldn't it? But I can't say I was thinking straight by the time I got to San Antonio.''

''Better now?'' Jane asked.

''Much better,'' he assured her as he reached for her.

Smiling, she slipped into his arms without hesitation.

"Then how about some lunch?" she offered. "I have a pot of Calvin's chicken noodle soup simmering on the stove. Or would you rather take a nap first? You look like you're wiped out."

"Soup sounds good, then maybe a nap. Just a short one. Otherwise, we won't have much time to work on the nursery. Unless you've changed your mind about doing that today since Emma's not here?"

Before Max had left, Jane had mentioned that his help getting the baby's room ready would be greatly appreciated. The walls of the spare bedroom—now used for storage—had been freshly painted the previous spring, but some clearing out and cleaning up were necessary. The baby bed had to be assembled, as well, and the other furniture they'd bought in San Antonio had to be unpacked from the shipping cartons, then arranged to the best advantage.

"Actually, I was cleaning out the closet when the doorbell rang."

"Not lifting anything heavy, though?"

"No," she assured him. Then she ducked her head shyly as she added, "By the way, thank you for the rocking chair. It's just beautiful."

"I'm glad you like it."

When Max had seen the old-fashioned oak rocker in a store window his first day back in Seattle, he hadn't been able to resist having the piece air shipped overnight. The gleaming wood had matched perfectly that of the furniture Jane had chosen for the baby's room. And gazing at the chair, he had instantly pictured her sitting in it, rocking gently to and fro, holding their child in her arms.

"I *love* it," she stated, her eyes shining. She hesitated consideringly for a long moment, then slipped away from him and stood. "Come on, let me get you some soup."

She hadn't added that she loved *him,* too. Not aloud. But Max wanted to believe the words had been on the tip of her tongue.

How he longed to hear her say them. Yet he knew he still had a way to go before that privilege would be his again. Over the past few weeks, there had been moments when he had thought he was close to winning back her affection. Then she would withdraw again, still too uncertain to trust him.

All he could do was show her—every chance he got—how much she and the baby meant to him, and school himself to be patient.

He would have liked to be setting up the nursery in *their* home, but he had forfeited that prerogative along with so many others. He wasn't happy about it, but living with the consequences of the mistakes he had made was the only choice he had.

Thankfully, Jane had never thrown the hurtful things he'd done to her in his face. But she continued to hold a part of her vibrant spirit inviolate. Even when she allowed him to hold her in his arms and kiss her, she seemed to be standing back, watching and waiting for the moment when he betrayed her yet again. And he had no words to convince her otherwise. At least none he could expect her to take at face value.

Max polished off not one but two bowls of soup along with several rolls while Jane sat at the table with him, sipping a glass of milk. She asked about his meeting in Seattle, then filled him in on the progress she'd made on her latest project—revamping the ad campaign for the HED laptop to appeal to a wider, more youthful range of potential buyers than Doug Jacoby had originally targeted.

When he finished eating, she sent him out to the car to get his overnight bag. Then, at her direction, he went upstairs, took a shower, put on fresh sweats and stretched out on her bed for what he again insisted would be only a short nap. Jane laughingly tucked Bruiser Bear in beside him, covered him with a quilt and left.

As the door closed behind his wife, Max hugged the fuzzy bear, wishing he held her, instead. Then, reminding himself that he couldn't always have what he wanted, he yawned, closed his eyes and within moments fell sound asleep.

Max wasn't sure exactly what woke him, and at first, he had no idea where he was. Focusing on the unfamiliar antique mahogany chest of drawers across from the bed where he lay, curled comfortably on his side, he gradually put together bits and pieces of the day past. He had been in Seattle, but he was back in Serenity now—at Emma Dalton's house, in Jane's bedroom there.

He had been worried about her, so worried that the flight to San Antonio, as well as the drive to Serenity, had been sheer torture. But she had been all right.

She had fed him soup, then sent him off to take a nap, he recalled with a smile, aware that he still clutched the baby's bear in his arms.

A glance at his watch told him he had slept longer than he'd planned, though. No wonder the light in the bedroom had faded. It was almost five o'clock. Outside, it would be nearly dark.

Yet he wasn't in any hurry to get up. He felt rested and relaxed, but he didn't think Jane would mind if he lazed a little longer. He would take her out to dinner to make up for being so useless. They could always work on the nursery tomorrow.

He set the bear on the floor, then stretched languorously under the quilt.

Yes, dinner somewhere…romantic, he decided, thinking of the Veranda's ambience. Maybe it wasn't too late to reserve one of the tables in front of the fireplace….

As his hip bumped gently against something soft and warm and nicely rounded, Max froze. Slowly, so as not to disturb his bedmate, he rolled onto his back and saw Jane, deeply asleep beside him. She lay on her side, her back to him, her bottom now tucked up against his hip thanks to his shifting.

For the space of a heartbeat or two, he could hardly believe his eyes. But the warmth of her body pressed so close to his, coupled with her enticingly feminine scent, quickly convinced him that he hadn't conjured her up.

Max had no idea how long she'd been there. Nor did he have a clue why she'd come to join him. He knew there had to be at least one other bed in Emma's house. But he wasn't about to expend any effort questioning his good fortune. Not when his wife lay next to him just as he'd dreamed she would one day.

Shifting again, carefully, Max turned so that he faced her. Then, ever so gently, he curved his body around hers, spoon style. She sighed deeply and leaned back, fitting herself up against him more intimately, then slept on.

Her silky hair tickled his chin, and her bottom pressed into his groin, causing him to swell and tighten as hot pulses of desire shot through him, but he didn't move away. Instead, he slid a hand over her belly possessively, and savored the sweet torment of her nearness.

He wanted so much more. Wanted to see passion flare in her beautiful blue eyes. Wanted to hear the sighs and whispers his loving could evoke. Wanted to give her pleasure unlike any she'd ever known.

But if holding her was all she permitted, it would be enough because it would also be another step toward the new beginning he had been working toward so diligently.

Chapter Eighteen

Jane drifted into wakefulness slowly, lured by the most delicious sense of contentment she had ever experienced. She knew almost at once where she was, and more important, who lay beside her on the bed.

She had worked at cleaning out the closet in the spare room for an hour or so after leaving Max to nap. But as usually happened sometime between mid- and late afternoon, she had grown sleepy herself. She could have rested on Emma's bed—her friend certainly wouldn't have minded. But Jane had been drawn back to her own room instead.

Just to check on Max, she'd told herself. To make sure he was comfortable.

Her first mistake—if mistake it had been—was to sit beside him on the bed. She had meant only to brush an errant lock of hair from his forehead, but before she knew it, she was lying down herself.

For only a few minutes, she'd vowed. Then she would go to Emma's room. Max would never know that she'd intruded.

Well, so much for that plan, Jane thought without the slightest trace of regret. She much preferred how things had turned out. Especially since Max didn't seem to mind her presence.

He hadn't jumped up and fled as if appalled by the idea of sharing the bed with her. Rather, he had curled around her protectively, splaying a hand over her tummy, stroking her with infinite tenderness.

She knew that he was awake, too. Had known instinctively since the moment she'd opened her eyes. Twisting slightly, she glanced over her shoulder and saw him watching her with sleepy eyes. He smiled slowly, sending a thrill of sensual excitement shooting through her.

"I didn't mean to wake you," he said, his voice low, his breath whispering warm against her ear.

"I'm glad you did."

She smiled, too, as she leaned back and undulated against him shamelessly.

"Oh, really?" he asked, a sexy glimmer lighting his gray eyes.

"Mmm, really."

"Ready to get up, then?" He eyed her questioningly, though he made no attempt to move away.

Jane understood what he was doing. Giving her a chance to stop what she had started before they went any further. But she had been longing for a moment like this for weeks now. She had tried to hold back, to keep some distance between them—both physical and emotional. Yet he had broken down her barriers with his unrelenting kindness.

Only when he'd left Serenity for his meeting in Seattle had she acknowledged how much she had come to depend on him. And as the days had passed, she had begun to regret all the times she had held him at arm's length. He had proved to her again and again that he was worthy of her love and trust, after all.

What better time to show him that than now? What better time and what better way...?

"Not unless you are," she said, lifting her head and kissing him on the chin.

"If we don't..." He paused, sucked in a breath, then moved his hand from her tummy to her breast and caressed her. "I can stop now, Janie. I don't want to, but I can. If we...if we stay like this much longer, though..." He hesitated again, then feathered a kiss over her lips. "I don't want to hurt you or the baby."

"You won't."

"Are you sure?"

"Dr. Harrison said that having sex was allowed until he advised otherwise," she told him, her smile widening.

"And he hasn't?"

"Not yet."

"So...?"

"So help me off with my clothes, will you?" she asked with a boldness that took her by surprise.

"My pleasure," he growled.

Max wasted no time undressing her, though he did so with exquisite care. When she lay before him, naked, he kissed her mouth, then her breasts, and finally, her tummy, his passion edged with reverence. Rubbing his cheek against her, he sighed deeply, then moved away from her just long enough to shed his own clothing.

Lying next to her, he eased her onto her side again—his chest warm against her back. Then he stroked her—just stroked her—over and over, as if he couldn't get enough of touching her.

The play of Max's clever fingers upon her, caressing her breasts and her tummy, then easing lower, gliding gently into her warmth, was almost more than Jane could bear. Pregnancy seemed to have made her body much more sensitive. Her nipples strained and ached at the slightest brush of a fingertip, and the teasing thrust and retreat of his delicate probing had her lifting her hips with an almost impudent urgency.

His breath rasped in her ear, and against her buttocks, she felt him, hot and hard—a sure sign that his own hunger was building. She twisted in his arms with a low moan, unable to put into words her sudden, desperate need.

"Too much?" he asked, his concern evident as he drew his hand away.

"Not enough," she whimpered, catching his wrist and holding him against her. "Not nearly enough…"

Shifting a bit, Max trailed a line of openmouthed kisses along the back of her neck and across her shoulders. Jane shivered at each exquisite lick of his tongue against her skin, arching back, then moving one leg forward, opening herself to him invitingly.

Max positioned himself behind her, then with infinite tenderness, slowly entered her. She whimpered again, leaning into his thrust, and took him into her, welcoming the pleasure of his penetration.

Moving slowly with a rhythm as old as time, Max lured her closer and closer to the edge. But she needed more, and he seemed to sense it. When the ultimate fulfillment she sought stayed just beyond her reach, he slid his fingers along the little nub hidden amid the silken folds of her feminine flesh.

Suddenly, wave after wave of boundless ecstasy rolled through her, and she cried out, the sound of her voice mingling with Max's as he, too, found release.

Long afterward, they lay together, wrapped not only in the quilt Max had tucked around them, but also in a sensual afterglow more sweetly peaceful than they had ever known. So long in coming had it been, neither of them wanted to break the spell of enchantment that seemed to hover over them.

Finally, however, Max stirred, albeit with obvious reluctance.

"So much for getting the nursery ready," he said.

Hearing the self-deprecation in his voice, Jane smiled as she snuggled against his chest.

"It's not that late yet. We could finish clearing out and cleaning up tonight, maybe even put the bed together, then arrange the furniture tomorrow."

"That we could," he agreed, hugging her close, then letting her go so he could lean over the side of the bed and gather their clothes from the floor.

"I'll have to eat something first."

Jane sat up and switched on the bedside lamp. She had thought she would be self-conscious about having Max see her naked. But when he turned back to her, the awestruck look on his face put any doubts she'd had to rest. As he had earlier, he bent over her and rubbed his cheek against her tummy, kissed her there, then again on her mouth.

"I wanted to take you out," he said, setting her underwear, pants and sweater in her lap, then moving away to don his briefs. "I imagine it's probably too late to get a table at the Veranda, though. Any other suggestions?''

''I'd really rather stay in tonight,'' she admitted.

She didn't add that she wanted Max all to herself for just a little longer as she dealt with her bra and panties, shimmied into her red sweater, then stood and pulled on her black knit pants.

''That means one of us will have to cook,'' he reminded her without enthusiasm.

''Not if we have pizza delivered. The dinner-hour rush is just about over, so it should be here in about forty-five minutes or so.''

''Sure you can wait that long?'' Max teased, coming around the bed to join her.

''Hey, I wasn't the one who gulped down two *huge* bowls of chicken noodle soup just—'' she glanced at her watch ''—six short hours ago.''

''Maybe not, but when I kissed you, you tasted a lot like those chocolate brownies with nuts and cream-cheese frosting I saw on the kitchen counter.''

''I admit I did have a little afternoon snack, but I really needed something to tide me over.''

''I'm not complaining. As long as you saved one for me.''

''Of course I did. I'm not *that* greedy,'' she admonished.

''Oh, no?'' A devilish gleam in his gray eyes, Max put his arms around her and kissed her soundly. ''Maybe not where brownies are concerned...''

Reminded of how wantonly she had behaved, Jane blushed, but didn't try to pull away. She might be feeling just a bit sheepish, but she was also rather pleased with herself. The emotions she'd expressed during their lovemaking had been deeply heartfelt. Just as she believed Max's had been.

"Lucky for you, huh?"

"Yes, very lucky indeed," he agreed.

They ordered a large veggie pizza, then finished clearing out the closet in the spare room while they waited for it to be delivered. When they were done eating, Max carried the boxes Jane had neatly packed up to Emma's attic. Then he set to work putting together the baby bed while Jane sat in the rocking chair and supervised.

After several false starts, Max finally figured out the supposedly simple instructions, and soon had the polished oak framework standing, solid and sturdy. He lowered the mattress onto the springs, then helped Jane make it up with the linens she had freshly laundered. At her direction, he moved the bed under the window, and while she decided whether or not she liked it there, he went to rescue Bruiser from her bedroom floor.

By the time he returned, holding the bear in one big hand, she had made up her mind to leave the bed where it was. Leaning over the lowered rail, she smoothed a hand over the pastel-colored, block-patterned quilt she had found at one of the shops along Serenity's Main Street. Then she stood aside so Max could put the stuffed toy in a place of honor near the headboard.

Watching Max tweak the bear's fuzzy nose, Jane was overwhelmed by a sudden, unexpected sense of remorse. They should have been preparing a room for their child in their own home, not in the home of a friend. And they would have been if only she hadn't been so suspicious or so stubborn. Now it was too late for that. Her due date was too close.

"What's wrong?" Max asked as he turned to face her.

"I should have gone back to Seattle with you in August. I should have believed you when you said you cared about the baby." She waved a hand at the crib. "This isn't fair to you—making you feel like an outsider...." Looking away, she swiped at the single tear that trickled down her cheek.

With infinite tenderness, Max drew her into his arms and kissed her on the cheek.

"First, you weren't ready to move back to Seattle in August. I understood that then, and I understand it now. After the way I treated you, you had no reason to trust me. Second, you haven't made me feel like an outsider. You've shared quite a lot with me, all things considered. Much more than I think I deserved.

"Yes, I would like for us to be in our own home, but we're not...yet. That doesn't mean we can't be together over the next few weeks, though—either here or at the Bergers' house. Then, once the baby's born, we can decide what we want to do next.

"Right now, however, I don't want you to worry about anything. I just want you to be happy. Can you do that for me? Please...?"

"I can try," she said, resting her head against his shoulder.

"Good enough." He kissed her forehead again, then took a step away. "Now, I think I'd better get going. It's late, and if I'm not mistaken, you were yawning just ten minutes ago."

"Don't leave," she pleaded softly, clinging to him. "Stay here with me tonight."

Somewhere in the back of her mind, she knew she

had reached the point of no return. The last of her resistance had finally drained away, and she was glad.

"Are you sure that's what you want, Janie?" he asked, his longing evident in his eyes, in his voice, in the brush of his fingertips against her cheek.

"More than anything." She stood on tiptoe and kissed the edge of his jaw, then added laughingly, "Well, anything except to see my feet again when I'm standing up."

"All in good time...all in good time."

He cupped her chin in his palm and kissed her with sudden fervor. Then he scooped her into his arms and, ignoring her protests, carried her back to her bedroom.

While Jane showered and changed into a long, ivory, brushed-satin nightgown with lace at the collar and cuffs, Max went to make sure the doors were locked and the lights turned off.

When she stepped out of the bathroom at last, she saw him sitting on her bed, bare chested, wearing only sweatpants and a sexy smile. He'd lit the small bedside lamp, but otherwise the room was deeply shadowed.

Without hesitation, she joined him on the bed, enticed by the mere thought of being held in his arms again, safe and secure. But once there, she lowered her gaze, suddenly, unaccountably shy.

"I have something for you," he said, tucking a finger under her chin, urging her to meet his gaze again.

"What's that?" she asked, unable to hide her curiosity.

"Something I've been carrying around with me everywhere I go for about eight months now. Something that I want you to have not only because you're my wife and the mother of our baby-to-be, but also because I love you more than anything."

Taking her hand, Max draped the gold-and-diamond bracelet he'd first given her on their wedding night around her wrist and fastened the clasp. As she had all those months ago, she stared at it, mesmerized by its delicate beauty.

"Please don't doubt how much you mean to me ever again."

Unable to speak past the tears clogging her throat, Jane went into his arms willingly. They had come a long way in the time that had passed. Far enough for her to hope for the best again.

Yet Jane couldn't quite forget the way Max had once betrayed her. Forgive, yes, but the *why* of it still haunted her. And with that came a tiny niggle of uncertainty she found impossible to discount.

Would he ever reveal his reason for walking away the night he first found out about the baby? Had it been something small and insignificant that he had easily set aside? Or had it been something much more serious—something that would resurface once the baby was born?

As long as Jane didn't know for sure, she couldn't be certain of how he'd behave a month from now when their lives would change irrevocably. She could only hold on to her newfound faith in him, and pray that she was doing the right thing. For herself, for her baby and for Max.

Chapter Nineteen

"Well, what do you think?" Max asked, flipping the switch that turned on the myriad tiny multicolored lights strung around the Christmas tree he, Jane, Emma and Margaret Griffin had just finished decorating.

"Oh, it's just lovely," Margaret said, her eyes shining.

Still recuperating from her chemotherapy, she looked a bit frail, but she'd been in high spirits since she and Emma had arrived a few hours earlier. Concerned about her elderly friend's well-being, Emma had decided to stay with her after she'd been released from the hospital just before Thanksgiving.

"Yes, lovely," Jane agreed.

Coming to stand beside Max, she slipped an arm around his waist as he reached out to hug her close.

With less than a month left before the baby was

due, she was moving much more slowly. She was also growing more uncomfortable thanks to her steadily increasing girth. Often lately, she'd been having trouble sleeping, too. Max knew because he had been staying with her while Emma was at Margaret's.

All to be expected, Dr. Harrison had assured them at her biweekly office visit a few days ago. He'd said, too, that the time had come for them to refrain from sexual intercourse. And much to Jane's dismay, he had indicated that—more than likely—the baby would arrive at least a week, perhaps two, past her December 23 due date.

Today, however, she had been buzzing around, busy as a bumblebee, dividing her time between the tree decorating in Emma's living room and the cookie baking she'd insisted on doing at the spur of the moment. Max had already made two trips to the grocery store, once for the ingredients she'd lacked for a batch of cinnamon tarts, and again for several boxes of the silvery wisps of tinsel icicles she and Emma had insisted they must have to finish off the tree.

"What about the angel?" Emma queried from her perch atop the stepladder.

At Jane's insistence, she'd had the honor of positioning the white-cutwork-lace-and-gold-spun-satin creation on the highest branch of the lusciously fragrant, seven-foot-tall Douglas fir Max had erected in a corner of the living room.

"A little to your left," Margaret instructed.

Emma made the slight adjustment, then accepted Max's hand as she hopped off the ladder. At the same instant, the buzzer sounded, calling Jane back to the kitchen to retrieve another pan of cookies from the oven—chocolate chip, if Max wasn't mistaken.

Watching as she hurried off, he shook his head in amazement. Just yesterday, she had spent most of her waking hours tucked under a quilt on the sofa, working lethargically on a report detailing her ideas for a new software brochure. Max hadn't really minded. He'd spent most of the day right there with her, doing almost as much dozing as she. But today, she seemed to be operating in overdrive, and he was afraid she might be overdoing it.

"I think Dr. Harrison was wrong, Max," Margaret said, a mischievous twinkle in her eyes. "But then, I haven't been putting much stock in what any doctor says lately."

"How so?" Max asked.

He knew that Margaret's doctor had used the words *cautiously optimistic* when talking about her prognosis. He also knew she was determined to beat the odds. But he wasn't sure what she had meant about Dr. Harrison.

"I'd say that baby's coming sooner than expected. Hope Jane has her bag packed."

"For a couple of weeks now," Emma chimed in. "She's definitely ready."

Max had to agree. Jane seemed to be counting the days now, just waiting for the baby to come, her excitement far outweighing any trepidation she might be feeling.

He, on the other hand, found himself breaking out in a cold sweat whenever he thought about what lay ahead for her—*really* thought about it in the dark hours before dawn when he held her close, rubbing her back, breathing in her delicious scent, savoring her vibrant warmth.

Women went through labor and delivery without

tragic results every single day. Odds were that Jane—and the baby—would, too. Yet Max couldn't seem to quash the panic that ate at his gut every time the subject came up.

"Good thing we had the baby shower last Sunday," Margaret continued. "She really was surprised, wasn't she?"

"And thoroughly delighted," Max assured her.

Although Margaret hadn't been feeling her best, she had helped Emma orchestrate the little get-together in Jane's honor. The other librarians had come, along with Trudi Berger and several of Margaret's old friends—women who had known Jane's foster parents, remembered her personally and were kind enough to contribute to the festive occasion.

Standing in the background, Max's heart had brimmed with happiness for his wife as she had opened the gifts meant for their baby. Her innocent pleasure at the generosity everyone had shown her had been his a thousand times over.

"What about names? Have you chosen any yet?"

"'Maura' if it's a girl and 'Blair' if it's a boy."

"Very nice," Emma said.

"What is?" Jane asked, joining them again, a plate of cookies in one hand, napkins in the other.

"The names you've chosen for the baby," Margaret replied. "Any preferences?"

"Strong and healthy," Jane stated decisively.

She set the cookies on the coffee table and started off again.

"Whoa." Max caught her by the arm. "Where are you off to now?"

"Back to the kitchen for the mugs and the pot of tea I brewed."

"You sit," he instructed, his tone brooking no argument. "I'll get it."

"Okay." She settled onto the sofa with a barely audible sigh, then called after him. "There's coffee, too, if you'd prefer."

Max did. He poured a mug for himself, then collected the tray Jane had put together and returned to the living room. While he'd been gone, someone had turned off the lamps so that only the glimmer of the tree lights chased the growing darkness. He set the tray on the table, then hunkered down on the floor, aware that Jane and Emma were eyeing him expectantly.

"What?" he asked, reaching for a cinnamon tart.

"We were just wondering when—exactly—Calvin was coming down," Emma said as she poured tea into the mugs.

"He's booked on a flight out of Seattle on December 18. He refused to wait any longer than that."

"That's what I thought," Jane agreed.

She exchanged a conspiratorial look with Emma, then the two of them shot a surreptitious glance Margaret's way.

"Don't even think about it," she warned. "I'm much too old and much too set in my ways for any matchmaking scheme you girls might have in mind."

"What do you think, Max? Wouldn't they be perfect for each other?" Jane asked.

"Only if Margaret agrees to move back to Seattle with us. I've invested too much time and effort training Calvin to let him go without a fight."

"*You* trained *him*?" Jane giggled. "Yeah, sure..."

"You know, I've never been to Seattle...." Margaret mused.

"Hey, getting them together might not be such a

good idea, after all," Emma said. "I don't want to end up living here all alone."

"You'll just have to move north, too," Max insisted.

"And leave my home?" Emma looked around her, sighed and shook her head. "I have almost everything I've ever wanted right here."

"Me, too," Margaret agreed. "But I might be talked into a visit."

"How about you, Em? Will you at least come for a visit, too?" Jane asked.

"As often as I can. I'm really looking forward to watching my godchild grow up." She reached over and squeezed Jane's hand. "I don't want us to ever be apart so long again."

"Neither do I," Jane assured her.

"You know, it's going to be lonely around here once the two of you go back to Seattle."

"Not necessarily," Margaret stated with a cryptic smile.

"Now don't *you* get any ideas about matchmaking," Emma cautioned.

"Oh, I've had ideas for years now. Just haven't done anything about them...yet." Margaret's smile widened affectionately as she met Emma's gaze. "Now, I think it's about time I headed home. Don't want to get too worn-out. My bridge club's Christmas party is tomorrow afternoon, and Wednesday there's the senior social at the community center."

Max and Jane saw Emma and Margaret out to Emma's car, then hurried inside to escape the chill wind that had started blowing late in the afternoon.

"Does it ever snow here?" Max asked, glancing at the dark, seemingly starless sky.

"Not very often," Jane replied.

"Feels like it might tonight."

"It's still pretty early in the season, and I don't think it's cold enough. We might get some sleet or freezing rain, though."

Max grimaced, hoping her forecast was wrong. Treacherous road conditions and power outages were two things he'd rather avoid having to face so close to Jane's due date.

"How are you feeling?"

"Pretty good, actually," she said, standing aside so he could shut the door and lock it.

"After all the running around you did today, I thought you'd be ready to collapse."

"Guess I must have gotten a second wind of sorts. Probably thanks to the fact that I did nothing at all yesterday." Frowning, she reached behind her and rubbed the small of her back. "Every now and then, my back feels kind of achy, though."

"Put your hands on the back of the sofa and lean forward a little," he said.

Jane followed his instructions, and he set about massaging the muscles along her spine as he'd learned to do in their childbirth class.

"That feels much better," she purred after a few minutes, straightening again.

Max put his arms around her and nuzzled her neck.

"Why don't you go upstairs, take a shower and put on your nightgown while I clean up the kitchen?"

"Talk about an offer I can't refuse…" She turned in his arms and kissed him. "But only if you promise you'll be up soon, too."

"On my word of honor."

Jane hadn't left much for him to do in the kitchen. The dishes from Sunday dinner had been washed, dried and put away, as had most of the bowls and cookie sheets she had used during her baking spree. She'd certainly had one heck of an energy spurt.

Again, the faintest flicker of concern edged into the corner of Max's mind, but he had no idea why. Jane hadn't looked any the worse for wear when he'd sent her up to take a shower. In fact, she'd had an air of expectation and excitement about her that he found a pleasant contrast to her moodiness of the past few days.

Dr. Harrison had told them emotional highs, as well as lows, were to be anticipated during the last weeks of a pregnancy. Perhaps Jane was just proving him right with her sudden shifts in temperament.

Thinking that she might be ready for a bedtime snack, Max brewed a fresh pot of tea, added some cheese and crackers to the plate of cookies still on the tray, then headed upstairs.

It was still fairly early—not quite nine o'clock—but over the past week or so, they had gotten into the delightful habit of curling up in bed together, each with a good book, and reading for an hour or so before settling down to sleep. Sometimes they talked, too—often about their plans to return to Seattle.

They wouldn't be having many more quiet nights alone, so the past few weeks had been a very special time for them—a time to get to know each other more intimately than they had ever had a chance to previously. Jane seemed happy about returning home with him. In so many ways, she had let him know that she, too, wanted them to be a family.

They had discussed the pros and cons of staying in the apartment versus buying a house a reasonable commute from the city, agreeing that a house would be better once the baby reached the toddler stage. They had also discussed the possibility of Jane returning to Hamilton Enterprises on a full-time basis. Neither of them had been enthusiastic on that score. But they had agreed she could easily keep her hand in by continuing as a consultant on special projects.

Despite the openness with which they had talked and the specificity of the plans they'd made, however, Max couldn't quite rid himself of the feeling that Jane was somehow steeling herself for the possibility that none of it would actually come to pass. For all the reassurances she had given him, he knew she couldn't quite trust him yet.

Obviously, the damage he'd done hadn't been completely repaired. And sadly, Max wasn't sure it ever could be. Perhaps over time, he thought as he walked into the bedroom. That was as much as he felt he had a right to hope for.

Jane stood at the bathroom sink, dressed in a long plaid flannel nightgown, a pair of wool socks on her feet to ward off the chill of the tile floor, blow-drying her hair. He set the laden tray on the dresser, then moved to the doorway, where he paused to eye her curiously.

"Weird, huh?" She switched off the dryer and set it aside, meeting his gaze in the mirror.

"You must have read my mind. You always wash your hair in the morning."

"Yeah, I know. But the oddest urge came over me when I stepped into the shower." Picking up her brush, she ran it through the dark, silky waves tumbling to her shoulders.

"You look so pretty tonight," he said, his heart warming as his gaze roved over her.

Jane studied herself critically for a long moment, turned sideways and rested a hand on her belly, then grimaced at her reflection.

"Pretty huge," she muttered, though not with ill humor.

"Not for too much longer," he assured her, putting an arm around her shoulders and urging her into the bedroom.

"Thank heavens for that," she breathed, leaning against him with a weary sigh.

"I thought you might be hungry." He gestured toward the tray on the dresser. "Anything look appealing, or do you have a taste for something else? A sandwich, maybe, or some fruit? Just say the word and I'll go raid the refrigerator."

Jane eyed the tray without much enthusiasm.

"Believe it or not, nothing sounds good to me right now."

"Not even a cup of tea?"

"Well, that would be nice."

While she got herself situated in bed, piling up pillows against the headboard so she could sit more comfortably, Max poured a mug of tea for her. Then he took fresh underwear, sweats and socks from the chest of drawers and went into the bathroom to shower.

When he returned to the bedroom not quite twenty minutes later, he found Jane lying on her side, eyes closed, her mug of tea untouched. He turned off the overhead light, then collected the tray and took it down to the kitchen.

Seeing that she was still sleeping when he came back, he crawled into bed beside her and switched off the lamp on the nightstand. Maybe tonight she would be able to get some rest. Considering how hard she'd worked, he certainly hoped so.

As he curled around her protectively, she sighed quietly and snuggled back against him. With a sigh of his own—one of deepest contentment—Max closed his eyes. Gradually, he relaxed as he matched his breathing to her slow, steady inhalations. Another day together gotten through safely, he thought. There wasn't much else he wanted or needed to count himself a lucky man.

Never a very sound sleeper, Max heard Jane get up several times during the night, but he didn't think anything of it—at least not enough to rouse himself completely. He had gotten used to her restlessness, and he now knew better than to fuss over her. The discomfort that had her out of bed, roaming around the house, also made her just a tad irritable. And she rarely wandered far—usually just to the nursery, where she would sit in the rocking chair and rock quietly, holding Bruiser Bear in her arms.

Twice when Max awoke that night—once just before midnight and once around three-thirty—he had the feeling Jane had been up for a while. But he trusted that she would alert him if anything out of the ordinary gave her cause for concern.

A glance at the clock on the nightstand told him it was almost seven o'clock when he stirred again. Gray light filtered through the slants of the miniblinds on the window, and rain tapped steadily against the glass. He stretched lazily, wondering how he would ever get back into the routine of working twelve hours a day at the office, then asking himself whether that would really be necessary.

He had proved he could run his company and still

have a life that included large chunks of family time. And he no longer needed to find ways to keep busy in order to hold bad memories at bay. The here and now was filled with possibilities too wondrous to miss. Like mornings lying in bed with his wife, listening to the rain fall.

Smiling, Max rolled onto his back and looked toward Jane's side of the bed. He had assumed she'd be back there, but she wasn't. Reaching out, he smoothed a hand over the sheet and found it cool to the touch. His smile fading, he tossed aside the quilt and sat up.

When was the last time he remembered her lying in bed? Shortly before midnight, he thought. Did that mean she had been up for the past seven hours?

Not necessarily. She could have fallen asleep in the rocking chair or downstairs on the sofa. He knew there was no need to panic, but he did feel oddly uneasy.

He swung his legs over the side of the bed, stood and started toward the bedroom doorway when Jane appeared there, an odd look on her pale face.

"What's wrong?" he demanded, immediately sensing her distress.

"I think…" She hesitated, braced an arm on the door frame and leaned forward slightly, massaging her belly with her hand as her gaze turned inward.

"The baby?" Max strode across the room, his heart pounding.

"Mmm, yes." She nodded, drew a deep breath and looked up at him again. "I think the baby's coming. I had cramps all night. Not bad. At least no worse than when I have a period. I assumed I was having Braxton-Hicks contractions. I got up and walked around, sure they'd go away. But they've been getting steadily worse the past hour or so. They're also coming closer together, and a few minutes ago my water broke—''

She paused again, leaning heavily on the doorway.

''Another one?''

''Yes,'' she replied, her whisper-soft voice laced with fear as she met his gaze. ''It's too soon, Max. Too soon...''

''Not dangerously so,'' he assured her, as well as himself, slipping an arm around her waist and helping her over to the bed. ''Let me get your robe for you, then I'll call Dr. Harrison and tell him we're on our way to the hospital.''

The moment Max had been dreading for almost four months had finally arrived. But as he saw to Jane's needs, called Dr. Harrison, then prepared for the drive to the hospital, an odd sense of calm settled over him.

Turning into a gibbering idiot wouldn't do Jane any good, and she needed him now more than ever, needed him to be strong for her. He couldn't transmit his terrible fear to her. Nor could he let it impair his ability to see her through the difficult hours ahead. The look in her beautiful blue eyes warned him that she was frightened enough as it was.

Max quickly changed into jeans and a sweater, helped Jane with her shoes and bundled her into her black cashmere cape. Though she said nothing, he knew her contractions were getting stronger. They were also coming about three or four minutes apart. Recalling what he'd learned during the childbirth classes, he realized she was already well into the second stage of labor.

Getting her out to the car proved to be a little tricky due to the rain, but he managed to settle her in the passenger's seat without mishap. He ran back to the house for her bag and—as much for Jane as the baby—good old Bruiser Bear. Then they were on their way.

"Doing okay?" he asked, reaching over to take her hand.

"So far." She glanced at him and smiled bravely. "How about you?"

"I'm okay, too."

At the hospital, a nurse whisked Jane off to be prepped while Max dealt with the necessary paperwork. They had planned to stop by and preregister after her office visit on Wednesday, never suspecting they might already be parents by then.

When he finished at the desk, they still weren't ready for him in the birthing room, so he went in search of a pay phone. Finding one, he called Emma—who promised to be at the hospital in thirty minutes or less—then Calvin.

Max was almost ready to hang up when the butler finally answered, sounding groggy. It was only then he remembered the two-hour time difference.

"Sorry, Calvin. I didn't mean to wake you," he began.

"That's all right, Max. Is something wrong?"

"Not exactly. I called to tell you Jane's gone into labor."

"How is she doing?" Calvin asked, suddenly alert.

"So far, so good. They're prepping her now."

"And you, Max? Holding up all right, too?"

"So far, so good," he repeated. "But Calvin..." He sagged against the wall, overwhelmed by a sudden sense of déjà vu, then continued in a shaky voice. "How soon can you get here?"

"I'll be at the airport within an hour, and on the

first plane to anywhere in Texas after that. With luck, I shouldn't arrive too much later than the baby.''

''Thanks, Calvin.''

''Take care, Max, and have faith. They're going to be just fine, and so are you.''

Max clung to Calvin's words as if they were an invisible talisman in the hours that followed. Along with Emma, he helped Jane through her labor, walking with her, rubbing her back, holding her, soothing her, even managing to make her laugh a couple of times.

She worked courageously and without complaint to bring their child into the world as naturally as possible. And at two-thirty on a Monday afternoon in December, she did just that in the hushed atmosphere of a room that barely resembled the one that had once haunted Max's dreams.

Emma was by her side, holding her hand, while Max stood behind her, holding her up as she pushed one last time, when Blair Elliott Hamilton—looking not the least bit premature at six pounds, two ounces and sixteen inches long—was born.

As Dr. Harrison held up the black-haired, red-faced, squalling infant for them to see, Max put his arms around Jane and blinked back tears of joy.

''Oh, Max, look,'' she murmured, her voice filled with awe as she reached out instinctively for her child. ''Our son...our precious little son...'' She took him from the nurse, then flashed a smile at Emma. ''Sorry, Em. You won't be able to buy those frilly dresses you love after all.''

''Maybe next time,'' her friend teased.

''Don't even *think* about that yet,'' Jane chided, cuddling little Blair to her chest, suddenly having eyes only for him.

"Congratulations, Mr. and Mrs. Hamilton," Dr. Harrison said. "Despite his early arrival, you have a strong, healthy baby boy."

Tracing a finger over his son's cheek as the baby rooted toward Jane's breast, Max felt his heart swell with love and pride. There had been a time when he'd thought happiness would forever remain just out of his reach. Now he knew differently. All he'd had to do was open his heart to the lovely woman gazing up at him with tears in her eyes, and let her make him whole again.

"I love you, Janie—you and little Blair. More than anything..."

"And I love you."

Chapter Twenty

Never in her life had Jane felt so loved, so cherished, as she did during the birth of her baby, as well as in the days that followed.

Max had stayed with her throughout the long, often tedious hours of her labor and delivery, his physical and emotional support unflagging. Emma had also been there, and between the two of them they had convinced her that she was capable of anything.

They had calmed her fears and eased her pain in ways that had touched her more deeply than mere words could ever tell. She had spent so much of her life depending on herself alone because she had been so sure she had no other choice. But they had proved that wasn't really true.

Dr. Harrison had insisted on keeping the baby in the hospital for observation a little longer than the usual postpartum period due to his early arrival. Since Jane had elected to breast-feed, she was allowed to stay, as well. And much to her relief—especially on the second day when little Blair started rooming in with her—so was Max.

Thanks in great part to the childbirth classes they'd taken, they had some idea of how to change a diaper and use a supplemental bottle. But Jane was so nervous at first that having Max there with her, teasing her gently and making her laugh, made all the difference in the world. He eased her initial anxiety greatly, relaying his confidence in her mothering skills in so many ways that she gradually gained confidence in herself.

Emma came to visit as often as her work schedule would allow, usually bringing Margaret Griffin along with her. And Calvin, calm and reserved as always despite the merry twinkle in his eyes whenever he spied the young master, as he had taken to calling the baby, lent his own special brand of moral support.

He made no secret of his pleasure in her newfound happiness with Max, giving every indication that he considered all to be right with the world now that they were together again. He also hit it off quite well with Emma and Margaret. Though Jane detected no romantic sparks between him and the older woman, their verbal sparring matches kept everyone including the hospital staff in stitches—so to speak.

Dr. Harrison finally released the baby on Thursday afternoon. Glad as she was to be going home to Emma's at last, Jane found herself overwhelmed by a new and different wave of uncertainty.

Caring for her baby with professional help only the beep of a call button away was one thing. Being on her own, even with Max and Calvin nearby, was something else altogether. She was the mother, the one most responsible.

Alone in her hospital room with the baby sleeping peacefully in his bassinet, Jane sat on the edge of the bed, still in her robe, clutching Bruiser Bear in her arms and feeling weepy for the first time since Blair's birth. The ''what if's'' she had been too exhilarated to consider suddenly piled up on her, exposing—at least to her way of thinking—just how inadequate she could very well prove to be as a wife and a mother.

''Hey, I thought you would be just about ready to go by now,'' Max said as he walked through the doorway.

Jane glanced up at him, then quickly lowered her head, swiping at the tears on her face. She had been so wrapped up in her fears that she hadn't heard him coming down the hall. And she hated having him see her cry.

He had done so much for her. The least she could do was pull herself together and try to do her part, no matter how formidable that now seemed.

The mattress sagged as Max sat down beside her and gathered her into his arms. She stiffened, resisting the comfort he offered, sure that she didn't deserve it, but he refused to let her go. Finally, she gave in with a tremulous sigh and leaned her head against his shoulder.

''Janie, sweetheart, what's the matter?'' he asked, tenderly stroking her hair.

''I'm not sure I can do this,'' she said, her voice clogged with tears as she toyed with the bracelet he'd given her.

She wore it always, as a reminder of his pledge to her. But today, it hadn't afforded her much solace.

"Do what?" he prodded.

"Be a good mother," she admitted sadly.

"You're already doing a fine job of that." He hugged her close, then planted a kiss on her forehead. "I'd ask our son to back me up, but the little guy's sleeping again. So it looks like you're just going to have to take my word for it. At least for the time being."

"I don't know, Max. All of a sudden, I feel so inept."

"You're not, believe me," he assured her. Then, as if sensing all that she'd left unspoken, he added, "You don't have to do it all on your own, either. I'm here to help, and I always will be. I promise I'll never abandon you again. Not under any circumstances. In fact, you couldn't get rid of me if you tried."

"Oh, Max..." Touched by his gentle, teasing tone, Jane laughed in spite of herself.

"I've taken care of the last of the paperwork. We're free to go whenever you're ready." He plucked the bear from her arms, then handed her the sweater and pants she'd set on the bed earlier. "Why don't you get dressed while I take the flowers and gifts out to the car?"

"Okay." She pulled a tissue from her pocket, wiped her eyes and blew her nose.

"We're going to be all right," he said, tipping her face up. "For now, and for always."

Jane nodded wordlessly, her gaze locked with his, wanting more than anything to believe that what he'd said would turn out to be true.

Once settled at Emma's house, Jane soon regained her equanimity. Max and Calvin seemed intent on seeing if they could outdo each other when it came to pampering her and caring for Blair. Some days, she wondered if she would have seen her son at all if she hadn't been nursing.

The rest they made sure she got and the healthy meals they insisted she eat soon had her feeling much like her old self again. Though she was still a bit sore and a bit tired, within a couple of weeks her spirits had lifted considerably.

She still had moments when the responsibilities of motherhood gave her pause, but she rebounded almost immediately. Thankfully, her tearful bout of post-partum blues had been only a temporary aberration. With the baby thriving, Max and Calvin treating her like a queen, and with Christmas just around the corner, Jane rarely had reason to remind herself of how truly blessed she was.

Emma had insisted they stay at her house as long as they wanted. She was quite content at Margaret's, and the older woman seemed grateful for her continued presence.

Jane and Max had agreed that they, along with Calvin, would remain there until after New Year's so they could all enjoy the holidays together. Then Calvin would return to Seattle and prepare for their return with the baby in mid-January after she and Blair had a last visit with their doctors in Serenity.

Perhaps not surprisingly, Jane had mixed feelings about leaving the small town. The months she had spent there had been filled with changes—the kind of life changes she had never expected to experience at all, much less with such positive results.

She now had a husband who loved her and a son who needed her. They were the family she had always wanted but had never dared to believe she would have. And they filled her heart with joy.

No moments were more precious to her than those she spent cradled in Max's arms as she nursed their baby. The warmth of his body so close to hers, the feather-light whisper of his breath against her hair, the stroking of his hand on her arm as the baby tugged greedily at her breast made her feel complete.

There was nothing she wouldn't have done for them. No sacrifice so great that she wouldn't make it. Yet some small part of her still quaked at the prospect of their special time together in this special place coming to an end.

What would happen when their interlude was over and their *real* life began again? Would Max still be willing, perhaps even *able,* to keep the promises he had made? Or would he be reminded of why he had originally chosen to distance himself from her all those months ago? Would he realize that he'd made another mistake after all?

Jane tried not to think that far ahead. But every time any mention of their move back to Seattle came up in conversation, the same agonizing questions whirled through her mind all over again. More and more lately, she would try to change the subject, and that, in turn, had Max eyeing her with bemusement.

One night just before Christmas, as the baby slept in the cradle Calvin had given them and they prepared for bed, he questioned her about it, revealing *his* concern.

"I've been getting the feeling that you're not very enthusiastic about going back to Seattle." Sitting down on the bed and drawing her onto his lap, Max spoke softly so as not to disturb Blair. But there was no discounting the directness of his manner. "Any special reason for that?"

Jane wanted to be honest with him. But how could she tell him that their return home loomed in her mind as the final test of his veracity? Almost five months had passed since he'd given her any reason to doubt the sincerity of his vows to her. And what kind of future would they have if she couldn't put the past behind her once and for all?

"I'm going to miss being here with you...like this," she said, settling for the partial truth as she leaned against his shoulder. "You've spoiled me these past few weeks. Once we're back in Seattle, you're going to be so busy at Hamilton Enterprises, making up for lost time and all—"

"Not too busy for you and Blair," he assured her. "The time away has shown me twelve- or fourteen-hour days, six or seven days a week aren't really necessary to run the company. That was just my way of filling the void in my life—a void that's gone now that I have you and Blair. I plan to be around a lot. In fact, you'll probably get so tired of having me underfoot, you'll be glad to see me go most mornings so you can have a little peace and quiet."

"I don't know about *that*," she murmured. "Having you underfoot has really been kind of nice."

"Hey, you're not just saying that to make me feel good, are you?" he teased.

"I'm saying that because I meant it, Max." Reaching up, she cupped his face in her palm and drew his head down so she could steal a kiss.

Contrary to what she'd read in the baby books, her ardor for her husband hadn't lessened after Blair's arrival. But Max had been adamant about following Dr.

Harrison's orders to refrain from sexual intercourse until after her office visit in January.

He couldn't resist her kisses, though. Any more than she could resist his. And in the past week or so, they had turned that particular way of mating into a truly sensual art form.

Whenever Blair allowed...

Her son's presqualling whimper had Jane easing out of Max's embrace reluctantly.

"I'll get him," he said, brushing her hair away from her flushed face.

He shifted, letting her slide off his lap, then stood and crossed to the cradle.

"Hey, little guy, Daddy's here." Max bent and lifted his son in his arms, and immediately the baby quieted. "Oh, somebody needs a change." He looked at Jane and grinned. "I'll get this one."

"Let me guess. Wet only?"

"I've done the honors with the other kind, too," he reminded her.

"Uh-huh." She offered him a wry smile.

"We'll be right back."

"I'll be here."

Clean and dry, the baby nursed contentedly, falling asleep in Jane's arms. She tucked him into his cradle, then hurried back to bed and Max's waiting arms.

When the baby awoke again a few hours later, Max got up to tend to him. He had taken over the 3:00 a.m. feeding so Blair would get used to taking a bottle, and so the two of them could have some special father-son time together.

Jane dozed, but as always, couldn't fall sound asleep again until they returned. The baby seemed fussier than usual, but she knew better than to intervene. Her presence made it more difficult for Max to get him to take the bottle, and her still-tender breasts needed the respite.

When it seemed the baby had been quiet for a while, but Max still hadn't returned, Jane crawled out of bed, curious about what was going on. She knew she would probably be sorry. Max had proved he was perfectly capable of caring for his son, and the idea was for *her* to get the rest her body needed to heal.

The glow of the little lamp in the nursery caught her attention, but when she peeked in the doorway, the room was empty. Turning away, she headed for the stairs, and crept down quietly in the darkness. Through the living-room doorway, she saw the glimmer of the lights on the Christmas tree, and knew that was where she'd find Max and the baby.

She told herself she'd just look in on them—hopefully without causing a disturbance—then go straight back to bed. But as she hovered in the doorway, the sight of Max, sitting cross-legged on the floor in front of the tree, gazing down at the baby he held so tenderly in his arms, held her still.

Jane had seen Max with his son many times over the past couple of weeks, but tonight there was a certain poignancy to the scene she beheld.

Under other circumstances, Max's visage could have appeared threatening. His dark, tousled hair and his five-o'clock shadow, his broad shoulders and big hands gave him a dangerous air. But the expression on his face as he looked at the tiny bundle in his arms revealed a love so heartfelt Jane wondered how she could be even the least bit uncertain of his intentions.

She continued into the room so quietly that he didn't realize she was there until she knelt beside him on the floor. He turned his gaze to her then, the look in his eyes changing, deepening, to express the equally strong, yet infinitely unique love he had for her.

How could this man have walked away from her that night in Emma's garden? She had to know. Otherwise, she would never understand, and thus, never be able to banish the last of her doubts.

"Why, Max?" she whispered, blinking back the sudden sting of tears. "Why did you leave when you first realized that I was pregnant? Seeing you with Blair..." She waved a hand in confusion. "I can't make any sense of it."

Max met her gaze for what seemed like an eternity without speaking. Finally, he looked back at the tree, now surrounded by piles of gaily wrapped packages.

"I was terrified," he said at last. "Terrified I would lose you the way I lost Alyssa. There were complications during her labor. The baby was stillborn, and she started to hemorrhage. Her blood pressure soared. She had a stroke and...and she died." Seeming to look inward, he paused, his mouth narrowed in a thin line, then continued. "Finding out you were pregnant..." He hesitated, shrugged, shook his head. "I didn't think I had the courage to go through that all over again. That's why I wanted our marriage to be childless.

"I never expected to fall in love with you on our wedding day or to create this little miracle on our wedding night." He turned back to her again, now smiling ruefully. "I thought I had it all worked out until you made me realize just how much was missing from my life. That first night at Emma's, I was afraid I'd end up watching you die the way Alyssa had. I thought I would be better off just walking away. But I couldn't do it because that was just as painful a way of losing you.''

''Oh, Max…I'm so sorry.'' Jane rested her cheek against his shoulder as tears trickled down her cheeks. ''I should have trusted you.''

''There's no need for you to apologize, Janie. You didn't know what was going on in my head, and I couldn't tell you without explaining about Alyssa. I didn't want to frighten you before the baby came, and afterward, I didn't want to spoil your joy.''

He had been thinking of her, *only* her, looking out for her in ways she hadn't even realized. And he had risked everything on loving again. Loving her and the child he held in his arms.

She sat back and brushed the tears from her eyes, then smiled at him. He smiled, too, as he gently shifted the baby to his shoulder.

''Come back to bed, Max, and let me show you just how much *you* mean to *me*.''

''Ah, sweetheart, I can't think of anything I'd rather do.''

In the bedroom, he tucked Blair into the cradle with a fatherly admonition to sleep for a while. Surprisingly, the baby did just that, giving his parents the time they needed to finally begin again, secure at last in each other's deepest love and trust.

Epilogue

Sunday, March 16

Dearest Jane:

I can't even begin to tell you what a wonderful time Margaret and I had in Seattle. Your generous hospitality made us feel most welcome. Thank you again for inviting us.

Your new home on Whidbey Island is just beautiful. I especially loved being able to help with the gardens. I know you will be happy there. It's the perfect place for you and your family.

Seeing you and Max together truly warmed my heart. You share a very special love—one you both deserve. And my godchild—what a little doll! I miss his sweet smile already, and I've been home only a few days.

On a more somber note, Margaret will begin another round of chemotherapy tomorrow. The fatigue she was experiencing during our visit was an indication that she's no longer in remission. I'm hoping the new drug treatment will help.

Margaret seems as positive as always.

She still refuses to contact Sam, but I feel like it's time he knows about her illness. I can't think of anything I would rather do less than ask him to return to Serenity. But he is her son, and he has a right to be here with her. Still, seeing him again will be hard for me.

Give the baby a big hug for me, and say hello to Max and Calvin—I have a pot of his chicken noodle soup on the stove as I write this! Also, please keep us in your thoughts and prayers, and I will do the same.

Much love to all of you,
Emma

* * * * *

Silhouette

SPECIAL EDITION ®

That's My Baby! ™

Don't miss these heartwarming stories coming to
THAT'S MY BABY!—only from
Silhouette Special Edition®!

June 1998   LITTLE DARLIN'
by Cheryl Reavis (SE# 1177)
When cynical Sergeant Matt Beltran found an abandoned
baby girl that he might have fathered, he turned to compas-
sionate foster mother Corey Madsen. Could the healing
touch of a tender family soothe his soul?

August 1998   THE SURPRISE BABY
by Nikki Benjamin (SE# 1189)
Aloof CEO Maxwell Hamilton married a smitten Jane Elliott
for the sake of convenience, but an impulsive night of
wedded bliss brought them a surprise bundle of joy—and a
new lease on love!

October 1998 FATHER-TO-BE
by Laurie Paige (SE# 1201)
Hunter McLean couldn't exactly recall fathering a glowing
Celia Campbell's unborn baby, but he insisted they marry
anyway. Would the impending arrival of their newborn
inspire this daddy-to-be to open his heart?

THAT'S MY BABY!
Sometimes bringing up baby can bring surprises...
and showers of love.

Available at your favorite retail outlet.

Take 2 bestselling love stories FREE

Plus get a FREE surprise gift!

Special Limited-Time Offer

Mail to Silhouette Reader Service™

3010 Walden Avenue
P.O. Box 1867
Buffalo, N.Y. 14240-1867

YES! Please send me 2 free Silhouette Special Edition® novels and my free surprise gift. Then send me 6 brand-new novels every month, which I will receive months before they appear in bookstores. Bill me at the low price of $3.57 each plus 25¢ delivery and applicable sales tax, if any.* That's the complete price, and a saving of over 10% off the cover prices—quite a bargain! I understand that accepting the books and gift places me under no obligation ever to buy any books. I can always return a shipment and cancel at any time. Even if I never buy another book from Silhouette, the 2 free books and the surprise gift are mine to keep forever.

235 SEN CH7W

Name	(PLEASE PRINT)

Address	Apt. No.

City	State	Zip

This offer is limited to one order per household and not valid to present Silhouette Special Edition® subscribers. *Terms and prices are subject to change without notice. Sales tax applicable in N.Y.

USPED-98

©1990 Harlequin Enterprises Limited

Christine Flynn
Susan Mallery
Christine Rimmer

prescribe a massive dose of heart-stopping romance in their scintillating new series, **PRESCRIPTION: MARRIAGE**. Three nurses are determined *not* to wed doctors—only to discover the men of their dreams come with a medical degree!

Look for this unforgettable series in fall 1998:

October 1998: **FROM HOUSE CALLS TO HUSBAND** by Christine Flynn

November 1998: **PRINCE CHARMING, M.D.** by Susan Mallery

December 1998: **DR. DEVASTATING** by Christine Rimmer

Only from

Silhouette®SPECIAL EDITION®

Available at your favorite retail outlet.

Silhouette® SPECIAL EDITION®

Newfound sisters Bliss, Tiffany and Katie
learn more about family and true love
than they *ever* expected.

A new miniseries by

LISA JACKSON

A FAMILY KIND OF GUY (SE#1191) August 1998
Bliss Cawthorne wanted nothing to do with ex-flame
Mason Lafferty, the cowboy who had destroyed her
dreams of being his bride. Could Bliss withstand his irresistible charm—the second time around?

A FAMILY KIND OF GAL (SE#1207) November 1998
How could widowed single mother Tiffany Santini be
attracted to her sexy brother-in-law, J.D.? Especially
since J.D. was hiding something that could destroy the
love she had just found in his arms....

And watch for the conclusion of this series in
early 1999 with Katie Kinkaid's story in
A FAMILY KIND OF WEDDING.

Available at your favorite retail outlet. Only from

COMING NEXT MONTH

#1195 EVERY COWGIRL'S DREAM—Arlene James
That Special Woman!

Feisty cowgirl Kara Detmeyer could handle just about anything—except the hard-edged stockman escorting her through a dangerous cattle drive. Rye Wagner had stubbornly insisted he'd never settle down again, but a daring Kara had *every* intention of roping in the man of her dreams!

#1196 A HERO FOR SOPHIE JONES—Christine Rimmer
The Jones Gang

Vowing to reclaim his father's lost land, ruthless Sinclair Riker embarked on the heartless seduction of beguiling Sophie B. Jones. But Sophie's sweet, intoxicating kisses had cast a magical spell over him—and he ached to do right by her. Could love transform Sin into Sophie's saint?

#1197 THE MAIL-ORDER MIX-UP—Pamela Toth
Winchester Brides

Travis Winchester fought an irresistible attraction to his missing brother's mail-order bride. Even though he didn't trust Rory Mancini one bit, he married the jilted city gal after taking her under his wing—and into his bed. But he couldn't stop wonderin' if Rory truly loved her *unintended* groom....

#1198 THE COWBOY TAKES A WIFE—Lois Faye Dyer

Sassy CeCe Hawkins was forever bound to her late husband's half brother, Zach Colby. Not only was her unborn baby heir to the Montana ranch Zach desperately coveted—and half-owned—but a forbidden passion for this lonesome, tight-lipped cowboy left her longing for a lifetime of lovin' in his arms.

#1199 STRANDED ON THE RANCH—Pat Warren

When sheltered Kari Sinclair fled her overprotective father, she found herself snowbound with oh-so-sexy rancher Dillon Tracy. Playing house together would be a cinch, right? Wrong! For Kari's fantasies of happily-ever-after could go up in flames if Dillon learned her true identity!

#1200 OLDER, WISER...PREGNANT—Marilyn Pappano

Once upon a time, tempting teenager Laurel Cameron had brought Beau Walker to his knees. Then, she'd lit out of town and left Beau one angry—and bitter—man. Now she was back—pregnant, alone, yearning for a second chance together. Could Beau forgive the past...and learn to love another man's child?

Chapter Ten

Jane couldn't recall ever being quite as shocked as she'd been when she looked up and saw Max standing in the doorway of the Serenity Library reading room. Not even when he asked her to marry him all those long months ago.

Granted, she had been surprised then, but…pleasantly. By comparison, the sudden realization that her husband had not only found out where she'd gone, but *followed* her, had shaken her to her very soul. So many weeks had passed that she'd thought she was safe.

When she'd met his stern yet searching gaze over the heads of the children gathered around her, her initial reaction had been fear. Not because she thought Max would do her any physical harm. She knew he wasn't capable of that. Rather, she'd been afraid of the emotional anguish he might cause her once he realized she was pregnant.

He had sensed her trepidation almost immediately, and had seemed hurt by it. But what had he expected instead? Anger, perhaps? Or joy? The tiny glimmer of joy intertwined with a faint ray of hope that had, indeed, underlain her anxiety?

As Max had turned to follow Emma, a dejected slump to his shoulders, the flutter of butterfly wings deep within Jane's womb had signaled her baby's movements.

Yes, little one, that's your daddy, and I *am* glad to see him, she'd admitted, resting a hand on her abdomen as she watched Emma lead Max away.

Why had he come to Serenity? More important, what did he want from her now that he was there? Jane imagined she would find out soon enough. But until she did, she wasn't going to say anything about her pregnancy. Thanks to her height, her naturally slim shape and the loose-fitting dress she wore, she knew it wouldn't be obvious to him.

Unless he already suspected…

Had Calvin hinted at where she'd gone and why? Was that why Max was there? The butler hadn't been pushing for a reunion lately, but that didn't mean he hadn't decided to take matters into his own hands in some surreptitious way.

Best to play it by ear, she had finally concluded, and assume Max didn't know about the baby until he indicated otherwise.

Offering the still-goggling children a reassuring smile, Jane had turned back to the story she'd been reading when Emma rejoined them. She indicated that Max was waiting for her right outside the door, then